Tui Street Tales

by Anne Kayes

SCHOLASTIC
AUCKLAND SYDNEY NEW YORK LONDON TORONTO
MEXICO CITY NEW DELHI HONG KONG

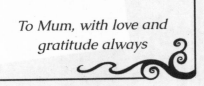

*To Mum, with love and
gratitude always*

First published in 2017 by Scholastic New Zealand Limited
Private Bag 94407, Botany, Auckland 2163, New Zealand

Scholastic Australia Pty Limited
PO Box 579, Gosford, NSW 2250, Australia

Text © Anne Kayes, 2017

ISBN 978-1-77543-472-6

A catalogue record for this book is available from the National Library of New Zealand.

10 9 8 7 6 5 4   1 2 3 4 5 6 7 8 9 / 2

Publishing team: Lynette Evans, Penny Scown and Sophia Broom
Cover and internal illustrations: Craig Phillips
Design: Smartwork Creative, www.smartworkcreative.co.nz
Typeset in Caudex 11/17
Printed by McPherson's Printing Group, Maryborough, Victoria, Australia

Scholastic New Zealand's policy is to use papers that are renewable and made efficiently from wood grown in responsibly managed forests, so as to minimise its environmental footprint.

Storylines Children's Literature Charitable Trust supports and promotes children's literature in New Zealand. For more details about this and other awards, and other Storylines activities, visit the website: www.storylines.org.nz

Contents

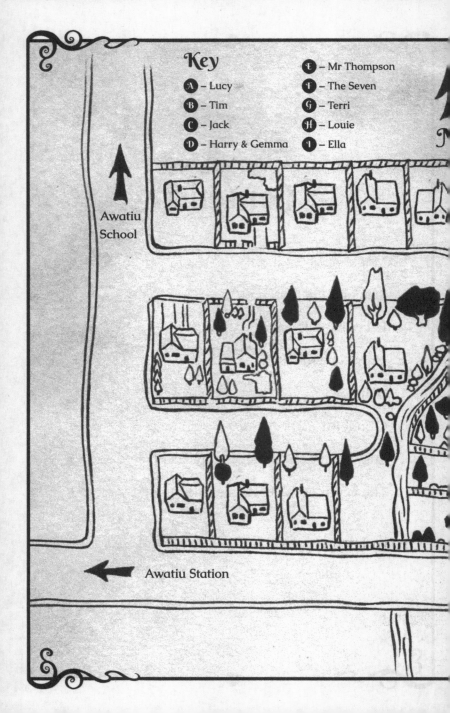

Motorway

Jack and the Morepork

IN FRONT OF JACK'S HOUSE in Tui Street grew a very tall tree. It stretched far up over the house and garden and way up into the summer sky; so far that no one could see the top. Each day, the tree's shadow spilled across Tim's house next door, like a long ink stain that shifted with the sun.

"Where do you think it ends?" Jack asked Tim one day, staring up through the branches. "Outer space?"

Tim stopped heading his soccer ball and shrugged. "There's a morepork in that tree," he said, looking up. "I hear it when I'm in bed." He began to imitate the peaceful hooting sound that often helped him fall asleep, "More-pork, more-pork."

"Yeah, I hear it too," Jack said. "Mum calls it a ruru." He frowned. "Don't think it'll last long though. That giant up there will eat it."

"Giant!" Tim scoffed. "Giants don't exist, Jack, and if they did, why would they be in a tree?"

Jack shook his head slowly. "Y'know that homework Mr Tāmati gave us?"

"The fairy tale project?"

"Yeah. We have to look for fairy-tale themes in our own lives."

"He didn't mean look for giants in a tree, Jack." Tim threw the soccer ball up and headed it so that it hit the tree trunk. "He said to think about how we deal with difficult situations, like how Rapunzel—"

"Nah, don't you see? My name's Jack ... and that tree goes into the clouds, just like a beanstalk. And then there's the ..." Jack faltered.

"The what?"

Jack looked around cautiously. "Come with me," he whispered. He led Tim through the front door of his house and into the kitchen. Quietly, he opened a drawer and pulled out a huge spoon, almost as long as his arm. "Mum bought this yesterday," Jack whispered. "It's too big to fit in a human's mouth."

Tim's mouth felt dry. "Well, it's a stupid project," he said. "Why does Mr Tāmati want us to study fairy tales, anyway?"

"Mum must know about the giant," Jack continued. "She's obviously feeding him."

"Feeding him?"

"Yeah, y'know how she does that with people," Jack answered. "Now it looks like she's feeding giants." He put the large spoon on the bench and looked at it. "This is fact three."

"What's fact one?" Tim's voice wavered slightly.

"Fact one's my name, fact two's the tree and now, this spoon." Jack sighed, putting the long, wide spoon back in the drawer. "The ruru's in danger, Timbo."

That night, Tim couldn't sleep. Each time he closed his eyes, the large spoon spun before him. Sometimes it made a clanging sound, as if clashing against metal ... or large teeth! What if there was a giant in the tree, hanging by his ankles from a sturdy branch, about to sandwich the morepork between his rotten-toothed jaws? Tim had to do something!

A sound at his door made him jump. "Tim?"

"Dad!" Tim let out a relieved breath.

"You okay? I saw you tossing and turning."

Tim sighed. "Dad, how do you know if something's a fact?"

Tim's father thought for a moment. "You have to prove whether something's true or not before you can call it a fact."

"So, if you think a large spoon means someone bigger than a human eats with it, that's not really a fact until …" Tim swallowed. He didn't want to hear the words come from his mouth.

His father finished the sentence. "It's not a fact until you see someone larger than a human actually eating with it. Otherwise it's just a guess, a hypothesis." He leant down to ruffle Tim's short, sandy hair. "Observe closely, Tim. That's the key to good detective work."

During the night, Tim woke often. Sometimes, he thought he heard the morepork calling. Sometimes uninvited giants invaded his dreams, their large toothy grins looming over him, feathers falling from their lips and clinging to their chins.

In the early morning, Tim woke to a tapping sound. Someone was outside his window.

"Fact number four," a voice called, "and five!"

Tim leapt out of bed and whipped back the curtains. Beneath Tim's window stood Jack in his pyjamas. His curly brown hair hadn't been combed and bits of it stood up on end. "Meet me in my back yard," he said. "There's something I have to show you."

Jack was standing underneath his clothesline, whirling it around. Tim had to weave and duck like a boxer to avoid being slapped in the face by dewy clothes. Despite his best efforts at avoiding them, a pair of Jack's mum's undies flew loose and hit him in the face. Jack laughed.

"Aargh! Get them off me!" Tim swatted them away.

Yanking the washing line to a halt, Jack's laugh faded. "Look at this," he said.

In front of Jack and Tim, with legs as large and wide as sleeping bags, a huge pair of blue jeans hung. Beside them were two enormous green soccer shirts, almost half the size of a soccer goal. Printed on the back of each was an orange number and name: 'Stratford' on one, and 'Rimu' on the other.

"I don't understand," Jack muttered. "Feeding a giant *and* doing his washing? He'll never go now. He'll stay in that tree forever."

With a frustrated push, he sent the washing line off

in another frenzy of spinning, clothes flapping wildly.

"What about the morepork?" Tim asked.

"It'll definitely get eaten."

From the kitchen window, Jack's father's voice soared across the whirr of the washing line. "Jack, what are you doing? Leave the clothesline alone!"

Tim reached up and brought the spinning spokes to a standstill. "Who are Stratford and Rimu?"

"Dunno," Jack answered, gazing at the huge letters. The R for Rimu was as wide as his chest.

Tim reached up and traced the letters with his finger. "Dad said it's not a fact until we have proof. It's just a hypothesis."

"Like in science?"

Tim nodded. It did seem as though Jack's mum was up to something, but they really had no clear evidence yet. Then he remembered, "Fact five? You said there was a fact five."

"Come with me," Jack said quietly.

Tim followed Jack around to the front of the house.

"Here," Jack said. He leant down and picked up some nails lying on the grass by the roots of the tall tree. "They haven't been here long or Dad would have mowed over them." His voice was almost a whisper. "Why would these be here?"

"Anyone doing any building?"

Jack shook his head.

"Fixing something up?"

Jack shook his head again. "Fact five."

"But it's not a fact until we can prove it. Your sister could've left these nails here. She always carries strange stuff around in her little backpack."

Jack shook his head. "Aroha can't reach the nails. They're on the top shelf in the garage."

Tim tapped his foot impatiently. "Jack, it's not a fact until we observe and get proof."

Jack looked up at the tree, then back at his friend. "Okay," he said, "let's make a plan." Slinging his arm around Tim's shoulders, they began to walk. "But let's do it at your house, Timbo. Mum will hear us here."

Because Tim's bedroom window offered the best view of the tree, Jack slept at Tim's house that night. Any contact with the giant, they thought, would probably be made under cover of darkness. Their plan was to stay awake all night to observe any movements near the tree.

Positioned at each end of the curtain, the boys watched the tree under the huge silver moon. As the night deepened, the morepork's soft chant began to weave its sleepy spell on Tim. His eyelids began to droop. Just as his head began to sink onto his chest, Jack's voice snapped him back to attention.

"It's Mum!"

Jack's mother was under the tree. She wore a woollen beanie with her long black hair tucked up under it. Clever disguise, Tim thought. A neighbour out for a late-night walk would never recognise her.

Checking quickly behind her, she pulled a torch from her backpack and pointed it upwards. Five quick, bright flashes of light bolted up through the branches.

Jack gasped. "A code!"

From the treetop, a rope ladder snaked clumsily down to Jack's mum. She grabbed it and placed one foot on the bottom rung. For a moment, she lost her balance and swung to the left. Then, straightening and checking around her once more, she began her second attempt. This time she stayed steady. With both feet firmly on the ladder, she began to climb.

"Fact six," Jack whispered.

Tim nodded, his eyes glued to the tree. Could Jack's mum really be climbing that tree in the middle of the night? His stomach lurched at the thought of what they should do next. "Jack, we've got to follow her now before that ladder disappears."

The hallway creaked as they tiptoed over it. Jack

bumped into a shelf, knocking over a photo frame. The clatter filled the silent house. Both boys froze. Surely Tim's dad would wake up! Jack imagined trying to explain this to him. A few heart-racing seconds later, they heard soft snoring coming from Tim's father's room. The boys let themselves out the front door.

Through the hot night, the boys ran to the tall tree. Hoisting themselves onto the ladder, they began to climb, rung after rung, higher and higher, until the houses beneath them were tiny matchboxes and Tui Street was just a thin smudge below. The higher they climbed, the more the ground disappeared, so that soon the only sound in the thin night air was the heave and rasp of their breath and the slap of their bare feet on the ladder rungs. Looking down, Tim felt his stomach twist sickeningly at the enormous black space between him and the faint lights of the world far below. Up and up, and on and on, as if the ladder might end at the moon.

Finally, above him, Jack stopped. "Listen," he whispered. Voices trickled down through the branches above. Laughter sing-songed through the night air.

"That's Mum," Jack said, climbing towards the sound.

The murmured chatter from above became closer and louder. Above their heads, they could see a wooden platform wedged between thick branches. Without hesitation, Jack scrambled up the last few rungs, clasped the edge of the platform and heaved himself up onto it, muttering, "Fact seven."

For the first time ever, Jack's mother was speechless. Her mouth dropped into a long 'O' shape.

The boys though, noticed only the giant. He wasn't ugly and toothless, like the one from Tim's nightmares. He was young, maybe even their age. His hair was dark brown and his large brown eyes were friendly. He sat with his back against the tree trunk, his long legs stretching across the uneven floor beneath them. Beside him, Jack's mother looked like a toddler. He wore the jeans and the green Rimu top from the washing line that morning. Pillows were nestled between the giant's head and the tree trunk. Jack noticed his mother had used the pillowcase with the koru shape on it that she'd bought from the school gala. Why would she use that one? It was her favourite.

"I see you've found us," Jack's mum finally said. "This is George, boys. George, this is my son, Jack, and his friend Tim."

George smiled and lifted his giant hand in a small

wave. Wincing, he lowered it onto his lap again. Jack noticed a large bandage wrapped around the giant's elbow. Even in the moonlight, he could see the bandage had pictures of Batman and the Joker on it. Batman's scrunched-up face gazed unevenly at him from George's arm. Jack looked at his mother. "That's my old Batman sheet. It was my favourite."

"We have lots of sheets, Jack," his mum replied. "Anyway, I'll wash it."

"I hurt my arm coming down the tree," George explained. The floorboards vibrated as he spoke. Leaves fluttered past Jack's face. George's voice was as large as his body.

"A couple of nights ago," said Jack's mum, "I was in bed when I heard a loud thud. I looked outside and there he was, lying on the grass."

"She helped me," George continued. "And she built this." He patted the floorboards.

Jack looked at the floorboards. Still annoyed about his sheet, it took him a moment to really notice them. "Nails," he said aloud. "Fact five, Tim. She used the nails to build this."

Tim nodded, still staring at the giant boy.

"When I was little, we were taught to always make people welcome in our house and on our marae," Jack's mother said. "I would've invited George to stay, but he'd have needed to slide on his side to get through our doors – and I was worried people might stare at him or tease him. In fact, you boys will need to keep this a secret." Turning to George, she explained, "Humans don't have much experience with giants."

"Can we just tell Ella ... or Terri ... or the twins?"

"None of them, Jack."

"What about Lucy? She's always making up stories and—"

"Jack, you mustn't mention George to any of the Tui Street kids."

"That's okay," Tim intervened. "We can keep a secret, eh Jack?"

With a frustrated snort, Jack nodded. Turning to George, he asked, "Why did you climb down the tree anyway?"

George smiled slowly, as if something special were appearing before him. His large face softened. "To see the bird," he said. "Just to see what it looked like. I wanted to see its colours, how big it was—"

"The morepork?" Tim interrupted.

"Yes. It helps me sleep at night. Our house is near where this tree pokes through the clouds. I just wanted to see what was making that peaceful sound, but now ... my parents must be so worried about me." One giant tear slid down George's cheek, making a small puddle on the wooden floor beneath them.

Jack's mum patted George's arm. "When his arm's better, he can climb back home. In the meantime, he's a bit lonely. You'd feel lonely too, Jack. Think of how much you'd miss Aroha."

Jack thought of his younger sister and how she often messed up his room when he wasn't home, and scribbled over his drawings. He shook his head. "I wouldn't."

Jack's mother's eyebrows rose. "I think you would, actually."

"I'd miss Dad," Jack said. His father told good jokes and coached Jack's soccer team. Yep, he'd miss his dad.

George interrupted Jack's thoughts. "Do you play cards?" he asked. Reaching into his shorts pocket, George pulled out an enormous pack of cards. Tim and Jack gasped. The cards were as long as a skateboard. On the backs of the cards were huge giant faces. "This is my new pack," George continued. "Got it for my birthday." He flicked through the pack, stirring up leaves and dust around them as he did so. "Look, the cards have got pictures of all my favourite soccer players. Rimu and Stratford are the best though."

Jack looked at Tim. "Rimu," he said.

Tim nodded. "And Stratford."

"Maybe we could have a game tomorrow?" George suggested.

"Lifting those cards?" Tim laughed. "Could be a long game!"

George's uncertain smile slid into a look of disappointment.

"But we could give it a go," Tim said. "Eh, Jack?"

"Wait!" Jack said. "Before we make any plans, I have to ask you something." He looked the giant boy in the eye. "George, were you planning to eat the morepork?"

George's eyes widened. "Me? No! It helps me sleep."

"Hmmm." He looked at George with a long, slow stare. He'd seen Mr Tāmati do this at school if he suspected someone wasn't being honest. Usually it made people uncomfortable enough to tell the truth.

George didn't seem uncomfortable though. Instead he smiled expectantly.

Jack began to speak, "Fact seven …"

"Jack," Tim interrupted. He put his hand on his friend's shoulder and lowered his voice to a whisper. "Case closed."

Recycling Ella

EVERY MONDAY EVENING, Ella was responsible for wheeling the family rubbish bins out to the kerb in Tui Street. Even when it was getting dark, she could be seen sorting through the rubbish, carefully separating the paper, plastic, tin and glass from the ordinary rubbish and placing them in the recycling bin.

Ella lived on the other side of the road from Tim and Jack. Although she took part in school activities with the other Tui Street kids, Ella

didn't often join in when they played soccer and skateboarded outside their homes. She'd wave at them, but her serious face seemed to say that she had other things to do, so the children waved back and left her alone.

Sometimes, if Tim heard Ella wheeling the bins down her driveway, he would join her, as he hated the thought of Ella working away by herself in the dark.

One evening, Ella's rubbish bin had a particularly nasty smell. Tim had to hold his nose. "What's in there? Smells like a dead rat."

"It *is* a dead rat," Ella said, scrunching up her nose. "The cat caught two water rats from the creek and brought them inside. Dad wrapped them in newspaper and stuffed them in this bin."

"Ew, they're rotting!"

"Yep. Sorry, Tim. You don't have to help me."

"Yuk!" Tim muttered to himself as he walked a few steps away to pick up a long stick from under a tree. "Why didn't he wrap them up more – or just bury them?"

Ella didn't answer. She'd become absorbed in fishing a large plastic bottle out of the bin.

"Here, use this," Tim said, holding out the long stick, "or you might accidentally touch one."

Ella worked quickly and quietly, passing pieces of recyclable rubbish to Tim, who stomped angrily on them before hurling them into the recycling bin. He couldn't understand Ella's father. After Ella's mother had died, he just left her alone a lot. Now, even with her stepmother and two small stepsisters there, she still often seemed to be alone.

After helping Ella with the rubbish, Tim went home to shower and get ready for bed. His dad looked up from his laptop when Tim came out in his pyjamas. "All cleaned up, Tim?"

"Yep. Definitely needed a shower after that. Their bin was gross."

"Well, no bin's exactly hygienic."

"Yeah, I know, but … Dad … does Ella's father like her?"

Tim's dad's eyebrows dipped downwards, as they often did when he was presented with something unexpected. "I'm sure he does. Why do you ask?"

"I think he's mean to her."

"Hmmm." Tim's father scratched his head. "He was very lonely after Ella's mum died. I'm sure he cares for Ella well enough, but I guess he found it hard being on his own with a child."

Tim shook his head. "But we're okay on our own."

"After your mum died, Tim, we had so much help

from your aunties and uncles – and Jack's mum and dad next door. They still help me when I need someone to mind you. I don't think Ella's dad has had much help."

"Jack said his mum tried to help, but Ella's dad was rude."

Tim's father raised an eyebrow.

"It's true – he told her to leave them alone."

"Some people just like to keep to themselves, Tim. He's entitled to do that."

"Yeah, but what if Ella doesn't like living that way?"

Tim's dad looked down at his watch. "Sit down, Tim." Tim sat on the arm of the sofa. His father leaned toward him. "I'm sure it was hard for Ella after her mum died," he said. "She was sad and she had a sad father who didn't want other people around. I don't think he's actually mean to her though. I've heard him be a bit gruff sometimes, but never cruel. I wouldn't stand by quietly if I heard someone being unkind to a child." The laptop made a beeping sound. Tim's father closed the lid and turned back to Tim again.

"I just don't think she's okay." It was hard for Tim to explain. "He kind of ignores her."

Tim's father tapped his fingers on the closed laptop.

"What about Ella's stepmother – Serena, isn't it? She seems friendly."

"Ella doesn't talk about her much."

"I'd hoped that when Serena and her little girls joined the family, it might be a happier home for Ella."

Tim stood up and walked over to the curtain, looking out across the road to Ella's house. The lights were on and the curtains were closed. From where he stood, it looked like any other house on Tui Street. "Her dad might be happier with the stepmother and her daughters, but Ella isn't."

Tim's father joined him at the window, looking over at Ella's house. "Have you seen anyone do anything that's clearly nasty to Ella?"

"No." Tim ran his fingers through his still damp hair. Then he remembered the rats. "Not clearly nasty to Ella, but not very nice either."

"Hmmm. I suppose the best thing you can do is be kind to, Ella and keep an eye out. If you see or hear anything that really worries you, then I need to know."

"Okay." Tim could feel his father's eyes on him, as he let the curtain drop back into place. "If I find any evidence, I'll tell you." He yawned. "Anyway, I'm off to bed. See you in the morning."

Tim's father reached down and tousled Tim's hair. "Goodnight, son."

The next day was a school day and Tim found Jack waiting for him on the front steps, fiddling with his shoe laces. "Morning Timbo," he said, standing and adjusting his backpack. "Got something for you – chocolate brownie. Three pieces each. Mum made it this morning." He handed Tim three still-warm brownies wrapped in lunch paper. Shavings of chocolate and dustings of icing sugar were sprinkled on top of each brownie.

"Yes!" Tim sniffed the brownie and sighed with pleasure. "Gotta tell you something, Jack, but we need evidence."

Jack's eyes widened, but when he opened his mouth to speak, it was full of soggy brownie.

Tim lowered his voice. "It's Ella."

Jack swallowed. "You mean Ella in our street?" he asked. "Recycling Ella?"

"Yep. Something's not right, even with the step-mother and her daughters living there."

Jack chewed quietly as he walked. "You know what this is, don't you?" he whispered eventually. "The fairy tale project."

"Jack …"

"Look at the facts. There's a stepmother, two stepsisters and an Ella, like Cinder—"

"It's not a fairy tale," Tim said quietly. He could feel a headache starting at the back of his eyes. Luckily, Terri jogged up to them with her soccer ball and they began passing and dribbling as they walked. By the time they reached the school gate, thoughts of cruel stepmothers and mistreated step-daughters had gone, along with Tim's headache.

Early that same morning, Serena had bought some small pizza buns from the local bakery. She'd hoped Ella might be excited at the thought of taking one for lunch.

"The buns just called to me through the bakery window," she said, laughing. "And I know you like them, Ella."

Ella was at the table eating toast and practising her spelling words once again before the test at school. She looked up briefly, before looking back at her notebook.

"We like pizza too!" Rita said. "Don't forget us!"

"I wouldn't forget you." Serena held up a pizza bun in each hand and made a point of showing her daughters, Rita and Angela, that she was placing them in their lunchboxes.

"I think I'd rather have my cheese and marmite sandwiches, thanks," Ella said quietly, without looking up. She'd always made cheese and marmite sandwiches with her mum. They had played a game called 'lining up the cheese'. They'd each take a piece of bread and see whose piece of cheese was cut the straightest, by lining it up against the straight edges of the bread. Ella usually won. Looking back now, Ella wondered if her mother had let her win.

Serena wasn't easily put off. She put the pizza bun in a small container. "Okay, I'll leave your bun for you to eat when you get home from school. You might feel like it for afternoon tea."

"Thanks," Ella said politely.

Getting to school had become a bit tricky for Ella. Before her mum had become sick, she used to walk to school with her. After she died, Ella had become used to her own company. However, since Rita and Angela had moved in, they insisted on walking to school with her, and frequently told her how much they loved having such a big sister. Mostly she wished they'd be quiet, although sometimes the things her stepsisters chatted about could be interesting, in a five- and six-year old kind of way.

That particular morning, Serena told them she

was going to walk with them too. She wanted to have a quick chat with Ella's teacher, Mr Tāmati. She had an idea she wanted to discuss.

"What's the idea? I can tell him," Ella said. "You don't need to come in." She wished Serena would stop trying to be involved in everything. She didn't need her help.

Serena shook her head. "At the moment it's a secret, because it may not even happen. Even if Mr Tāmati likes the idea, I might keep it as a surprise. Surprises can be fun." Serena reached out and squeezed Ella's shoulder.

Ella shrugged to show she didn't mind either way, but also to shake Serena's hand off her shoulder.

When Serena arrived at Ella's classroom door, she scanned the room. Spotting Ella sitting on a cushion reading in the library corner, she gave her a little wave as if casting a spell with a wand. Ella nodded at Serena and then looked down at her book, hoping she'd realise she was busy reading. Fortunately, Serena walked straight to Mr Tāmati's desk and sat down beside him.

Ella couldn't hear what they were saying, but she could see Mr Tāmati doing a lot of nodding. Small pieces of the conversation drifted her way.

She heard Serena mention the word "rubbish" twice and "recycling" once. She also heard Mr Tāmati say, "I wanted to do a special art project with them this term and your idea will be perfect." Serena's response though, was lost through the squeaking of a chair and someone dropping books on the floor.

The conversation seemed to be ending. Serena stood, smiled and said a few more words. Mr Tāmati smiled back and said, "See you Monday at eleven then – straight after morning tea."

As Serena made her way out of the room, she turned, did her wand-like wave at Ella and mouthed, "See you later." Then she was gone.

Ella stared at the words on the page in front of her. What special art project had Serena been organising with Mr Tāmati? Why did she have to stick her nose in school stuff? Wasn't it enough that she'd brought two small girls and pizza buns into Ella's house?

That night at the dinner table, Ella's dad pointed to a bump on his forehead. "I miscalculated the height of a doorway at work today," he explained. He was a tall man, who often had to duck his head to get through doorways.

"Your height was the first thing I noticed about

you," Serena said. "You were so tall that it seemed as if your head could touch the stars while your feet stayed on the earth."

Ella was struck by a memory. "Dad, remember when Mum was alive and you two were talking in the kitchen? I was in bed and I heard Mum say, 'I had to marry you, Bob, because your head's in the clouds and you need me to check your shoes are on the right feet before you go to work.' D'you remember?"

Ella's father nodded. "Yes, I do." He looked down at his plate. When he looked up, he said, "So, tell me, have you three girls had a good day at school?"

Ella didn't care that he was trying to change the subject. She remembered it all very well. After her mother had said that, her dad's laugh had risen, air-filled and warm like a hot-air balloon, and floated through the house. Ella had smiled in bed, picturing his face, his crinkled eyes, his laughter as easy as his breath. She liked the way her mum joked with her dad about how dreamy he was. Her mother, on the other hand, was so organised. No one needed to worry when she was around. The fridge always had milk in it. The washing was hung out. The cheese always lined up with the bread.

On the following Monday, Serena waved Ella, Rita and Angela off to school. "See you at eleven o'clock, Ella," she said. "I'll be helping Mr Tāmati with the surprise."

"It's not really a surprise," Ella retorted. "I already know it's an art project."

Serena smiled. "Ah, yes, but what exactly is it?" She tapped her nose. "I knows!" She turned away and walked back into the house.

Ella didn't like surprises. Surprises could be nasty … like her mother getting sick. When her mum's legs started crumpling beneath her, the doctors said the x-rays showed a brain tumour. Within days, a van had delivered a wheelchair. Her mum hated it and Ella often snuck it out of her room while she snoozed.

Her mother began to spend more and more time in bed. The minute Ella was home from school, she'd go straight to her parents' bedroom. "Jump up," her mother would say, patting the bed. "Tell me about your day. How did the spelling test go?" She always asked questions. Had the speech gone well? Had she eaten her lunch? Had Dad lined up the cheese?

Ella tried to think of funny things to say to keep her mother away from the sadness. Perhaps she might even get better if she laughed enough.

Soon Ella's mum almost completely stopped speaking. Ella would lie beside her and chat anyway. She'd explain how she'd forgotten to introduce the topic of her speech or how she'd left her spelling notebook at home. It was getting harder to think of funny things to say.

Sometimes, Ella's mum reached over and patted her as if she were a cat. Often, though, her eyes stayed closed. With a deep, concentrated breath, she might ask Ella about Tim, Jack or other children in the street, or ask whether the feijoas were growing on the trees outside yet.

Her dad said her mum was going to die, but Ella felt in a very small way that she might not. Sometimes magical things could happen.

Now she knew better. She also knew how she felt about surprises.

During morning tea, Ella played on the obstacle course with her friend Lucy. She kept an eye out for Serena, while Lucy chatted about a story she was writing.

"It's about a princess visiting Tui Street," she explained, "for my fairy-tale project."

Ella nodded, but it was hard to focus.

Serena arrived in the car, which was unusual

because she liked to walk. Her car was a kind of round shape, like the belly of a plump man. Serena called the car Pumpkin because it was an orangey-yellow colour too. The car was filled with boxes. Serena climbed out and piled some of the boxes on top of one another and began to carry them to Ella's classroom. Mr Tāmati came back out with her and collected more boxes.

"What's in them?" Lucy asked.

"Dunno," Ella replied.

Lucy jumped down from the monkey bars, landing with a spongey thud on the safety matting beneath. "Let's help carry them, then we'll find out."

"No!" Ella was a little louder than she'd meant to be. "I don't want to help."

"Okay, well you stay here and I'll go. I want to know what's in those boxes."

When the bell went, Ella met Lucy at the classroom door. "You'll never believe it," Lucy said. Her face was alive with the energy of a secret bursting to be told. "Your mother—"

"Stepmother," Ella interrupted. "Serena."

"Yeah, that's right. Your stepmother, Serena, has got boxes filled with rubbish. Look!" Lucy took Ella by the elbow and led her around the classroom.

The tables had been pushed together and were covered in newspaper. On top of this lay mounds of recyclable household items: plastic yoghurt containers, milk containers, long pieces of cardboard, jars, lids, trays, bottletops, used envelopes and much, much more.

At first, Ella was simply struck by the amount of stuff that had come from the boxes. Then she noticed that the strawberry yoghurt was the exact one they ate every morning. The yellow-lidded milk with the calcium sign on the front was the one her dad liked to drink. The ice cream that said 'no preservatives or artificial colours' on its container was the brand Serena always bought. These recyclables were from her recycling bin. The strange thing was that each container was sparkling clean and had returned to its original shape, as if it had never been crushed by her and Tim.

Ella looked over at Tim, sitting opposite her. Surely he would notice that this recycling came from her house. Tim, though, was more interested in the tower Jack was building beside him. Layer by layer, Jack placed recyclable products on top of one another. Tim had just passed Jack a plastic tomato paste container to balance on the jam jar, when Mr Tāmati's hand landed on the jar first.

"I think that's as tall as we'll make it, Jack," he said quietly. "There's Lego if you want to make towers later, but right now, we're focusing on a different kind of creative project. Serena's about to explain it to you." Looking around the faces of the students in his class, Mr Tāmati continued: "Today, everyone, we will be working on something special. Serena will explain. You'll need to listen very carefully." Mr Tāmati looked at Serena and smiled.

Ella breathed out slowly. Thank goodness Mr Tāmati hadn't mentioned that Serena was her stepmother.

Serena stepped forward. Her long, brown-gold hair was swept back into a ponytail. Her blue eyes kept respectfully away from Ella. When she lifted her arm, a tinkling sound came from the bangles around her wrists. She spoke gently, as if the children were already her friends. Ella looked around the faces of her classmates. The whole class was giving her their full attention. Ella began to listen to what Serena was saying.

"We're going to make something from all of these things that have been thrown away. The recyclable stuff is on the table in front of you," Serena said. Then she pointed to the back of the room. "And in the boxes over there, you'll find other things that are not recyclable. These things would have gone into a landfill – massive rubbish pits in the ground – but you're going to create a piece of art from all of this instead. There's some very thick cardboard on Mr Tāmati's desk that you can use as well, and I'll bring more rubbish in tomorrow."

Students began to move restlessly in their seats; some even stood up, about to rush to the piles of thick cardboard at the front. Serena laughed. "Hang on! Stay in your seats. I haven't quite finished yet. There are more exciting things you need to know. Mr Tāmati has the glue gun ready to go at his desk. You can only use that under our supervision. There are paints on either end of this table."

Serena stopped speaking and slowly looked around the faces of the children seated in front of her. Everyone had become surprisingly quiet. "This is the most exciting bit, everyone. When the art pieces are finished, we thought we might exhibit them in the school hall and invite parents to come and look at them." She smiled at the class. "Okay, you've been very patient. Now, please make your way to Mr Tāmati – don't all rush at once – to collect the cardboard."

While the class busied themselves up the front, Ella gazed at the rubbish, mesmerised by its gleam and sparkle.

"This is all your rubbish," Tim said, sidling up to Ella.

Ella nodded. "And it's so clean."

"Like it's been through some kind of car wash or something." Tim picked up a piece of flat, smooth aluminium foil. "And how does it go back to its normal shape?"

Ella bent down over one of the boxes and pulled a silver cat meat pouch out of it. Lifting it to her nose, she sniffed. Flipping it over, she sniffed it again. "It even smells really good ... like lemon."

Tim picked up a polystyrene meat tray and held it to his nose. "This smells like ... a rose! Honestly, smell that." He held it under Ella's nose.

"How did she do that? How do you clean stuff like this so that it looks new and smells like perfume?" Ella lifted a puzzled eyebrow.

Tim dropped the rose-fragranced meat tray back into the box. "Dunno."

"She must do it after we've sorted out the rubbish. It'd take ages to wash and dry it. She must stay up half the night!"

"Maybe."

"Well, how else would she change dirty rubbish into ... this?" Ella swept her arm over the boxes.

"Dunno." Tim scanned the rubbish in front of him.

"Dad says the way to find out the facts is to observe. Maybe we should observe her."

Ella nodded. "Okay. She said she'll bring more rubbish in tomorrow."

"So she'll clean the rubbish tonight," Tim said, "after we've sorted through it, cos it's collection day tomorrow."

"So we watch her tonight."

"Yep. I want to know how she did this." Without thinking, the words that had troubled Tim came out. "Is she ever mean to you?" he asked.

"Serena?" Ella asked, looking at Tim with her serious eyes. "No, she's not mean to me."

Tim looked away, his cheeks flushed. "We'll need Jack's help too. He's good with facts."

"Need me for what?" Jack appeared with a large square of cardboard.

"Tell you later. We'd better go and get our cardboard," Ella said, heading to the front of the room.

Tim hung back and whispered quietly to Jack, "You're right. There's something strange about Ella's stepmother, but not like we thought. Ella said she's not mean to her."

"She could be lying."

"Ella? Nah, she was telling the truth," Tim said. "It's just ... Serena's ..." Tim stroked his neck. His throat was beginning to hurt. "She's not like other mothers."

Jack looked over at Serena, who was discussing art materials with a child. "She seems nice."

"Yeah," Tim agreed. "Uh-oh, Mr Tāmati's looking at me. I'd better get my cardboard." He moved away up the room, just as the teacher called out, "Tim, it's time you got started."

The moon was low. Its bony elbows of light nudged the green bins set out on the kerbs like messy Lego pieces. Some were overflowing, heaped with the unwrappings, unstickings and peelings of everyone's lives.

Crouched behind Tim's bins, the children could see Serena's comings and goings through the thin curtains. Her shadowy shape moved around the girls' bedroom, bending, straightening and gesticulating to her daughters in front of her. The children watched as she stroked the head of one of the little girls. A moment later, she leant down and disappeared from view under the window ledge.

"Damn," Jack muttered. "We've lost her."

"She must be reading them a story," Ella explained.

"How long will that take?" Tim asked, coughing.

"Not long. She reads to them every night." Ella

hoped she was right. Sometimes, Serena got so comfortable snuggling up with her daughters that she fell asleep.

Tim coughed again. "I'm not allowed to stay out too late cos of my cold," he said. He could hear the frustration in his voice. He had waited for this moment all day – the moment the truth about Serena would unfold. He needed to see everything. Did she close the door behind her quietly so no one noticed her leaving? Did she inch her way to the end of the driveway in the shadows? Did she aim straight for the bins or did she walk for a while first to avoid attention? He hated not knowing. It made his throat ache even more.

Jack nudged Tim. "Might be better if you go inside anyway. If you cough, she'll hear you and that'll ruin everything."

"I won't cough. Promise."

"Sshh!" Ella pointed at her house. Serena had opened the lounge window and was leaning out and looking around the front garden, as if listening for something. She placed her thumb and finger in her mouth and made a gentle whistling sound.

Everything was still.

Again Serena whistled, but this time with a bit more volume.

From the shadows came soft footsteps, small thuds, scrapes and the rustles of leaves, as tiny figures stepped out from behind pot plants, a bucket, shrubs, bushes and rocks. One jumped out of the letterbox and another came from behind Ella's bike propped up against the side of the house. It was hard to make out exactly what they looked like from behind the bins on the other side of the road, but the figures were definitely human, and, Tim estimated, about half the size of his cat! On their heads were floppy, cone-shaped hats. They wore raggedy coats with patches on them, and their legs disappeared into boots that curled up like an old man's moustache.

Ella's eyebrows lifted. "Gnomes?"

"Dunno," Jack answered. "Elves? What's the difference anyway?"

Ella shrugged. "At Christmas, it's elves. They wrap the presents at the North Pole."

"And then there's that old shoemaker who has those elves that made shoes every night," Tim added. "Hey, look!"

The small figures came to a stop under the window and looked up at Serena, who smiled at the gathering below her. "Hello, friends," she said quietly. "Thank you for coming to help me again."

A gentle murmur could be heard, until one small man, with ginger curls spilling from his floppy green hat, stepped forward and bowed his head slightly. "We are honoured. This is indeed a special task."

Serena's smile widened. "Thank you, Albert. You're very kind. You could charm the birds out of the trees!"

The crowd of small people murmured again, nodding heads.

"You should talk to my wife, Serena," Albert said, hand on his chest. "She thinks I'm charming too!" He smiled and the moon glinted on his teeth.

Soft laughter rippled through the group.

A small woman with a scarf wrapped around her head sidled up to Albert and poked him playfully on the arm. "Do I now, Albert? You'd be a lot more charming if you stopped talking and let us get on with Serena's task." The tiny woman looked up at Serena, her green eyes twinkling with merriment. "You go ahead now, Serena, and I'll keep him quiet."

"Thank you, Maggie," Serena said, smiling. "Well, the job's the same as last week and the week before. And when all the useful rubbish and recycling are sparkling clean, just stick them in the boxes in the garage." She looked at her watch. "I'll go in and check on the girls. Won't be long."

43

Serena began to walk away from the window then turned back briefly. "Oh, and if you find any rats, just do the usual with them. I must talk to my husband about the way he throws them into the bin like that. It's really not fair on Ella."

Light as ballet dancers and quick as Olympic sprinters, the smallest people Ella had ever seen leapt into action. Some high-jumped to the top of the bins, lifted the lids and, as if throwing Frisbees, plucked out the rubbish and sent it soaring down to the others. The people below were ready for action: out of their pockets they pulled small brushes, rags, polishes and detergents. They quickly assembled into small teams. The one at the front of each team caught the rubbish and passed it on to the next, who scrubbed it with detergent. The next one rinsed, the next dried, the next polished and the final one placed it carefully into a box from the garage. As each piece of rubbish made contact with a tiny hand, a brief, soft light glowed and the rubbish returned bit by bit to its original shape. While the little people worked, they hummed or whistled. Some showed off, doing the odd cartwheel or juggling the rubbish that flew from the bins.

"Who could be that happy, cleaning?" Jack wondered aloud.

"Especially cleaning rubbish!" Tim agreed.

"They're part of a team. They belong together." As she said it, Ella knew she'd said something from a part of her she couldn't explain. Her mum and dad had been a team with her. It was why she couldn't let Serena's smiles and pizza buns win her friendship. By the time Serena came back outside, just ten minutes later, the boxes were full of gleaming, sterilised, perfectly-shaped and sweet-smelling rubbish. "Wow!" she said. "You guys are kind to me. Thank you."

"We separated the recyclables from the ordinary rubbish, just like last time," one of the younger little people explained. She was probably around Ella's age. On her head, she wore a bandana and her coat sleeves were rolled up.

"Wonderful, Martha," Serena replied. "I can't tell you how grateful I am. I knew you'd be able to help me, even if it is a crazy plan. And, of course, it may not work."

A little old person stepped up to Serena, who towered over him like a giant. He stroked his smoky-grey beard as he spoke. "How's the plan going?" he asked. "Any success yet?"

"Not exactly. She's very clever though, and so talented at art. I try to talk to her about her art,

Archie, but she doesn't say much."

"Keep trying," Archie said. He reached up to pat Serena comfortingly. Her knee was as high as his arm could reach. "Never give up on a child."

The group of small people murmured in agreement. Serena wiped her eye.

Was she crying? Ella looked uncertainly at the boys.

Tim was already looking at her. "She's talking about you," he whispered. "She thinks you're clever and talented."

Ella nodded slowly.

"So," Jack added, "she's not an evil stepmother. She's not wicked at all." He turned to Tim. "Another fact, I guess. I'm confused." He turned to Ella. "Are your two little stepsisters horrible to you?"

Ella shook her head. "They're okay."

"They've gone!" Tim whispered loudly. "Look, they've all gone!"

Across the road, Ella's front yard was empty again, except for Serena, who stood alone, arms folded, looking at the boxes. With a sigh, she began dragging them to her car, lifting them one by one into the boot. If Ella strained her ears, she could hear Serena humming the same tune the little people had hummed. The melody seemed to perk Serena up.

Locking the car, she continued to hum as she made her way back to the house. When she reached the door, she turned and looked over at Tim's house, past the children hiding behind the bins.

"I wonder if I should pop over to collect Ella," Serena said aloud. "Guess she'll be home soon. Must be nearly Tim's bedtime." Turning back, she opened the door and disappeared into the house.

Jack stood up. "Pins and needles in my feet," he said.

Tim stretched and coughed. His front door opened and his dad stepped out onto the front porch. "Tim, that cough's getting worse. Time for bed."

"Coming, Dad," Tim answered, but he didn't move.

"She said you're clever," Jack said. "We got this so wrong. Who's wicked then?"

Ella answered, "None of them. They all try to be kind to me."

"But ..."

"Maybe this is different to the fairy tale, Jack," Tim interrupted.

"But if everyone's kind to you, Ella," Jack continued, "why aren't you happy?"

Ella didn't answer.

Tim's dad's voice cut through the silence. "Tim. Home. Now."

"I'd better go."

"Me too," Jack said.

"See you tomorrow," Ella said. She crossed the road, looking at her house. Somehow it looked lighter, as if the group of little people had carried something worrying away with them.

The finished artworks were hanging on the walls of the school hall. Each piece had the signature of the artist at the bottom. Families wandered around the hall slowly and thoughtfully. All of the Tui Street kids were there: Jack, Tim, Terri, Lucy, Louie, the twins – Gemma and Harry – as well as Ella. Small children ran around, but even they slowed occasionally to peer at a particular piece of art.

Ella had made her way around the whole exhibition twice. There were a few pieces she particularly liked. Louie, who was new to their street and school, had made a tui using real feathers. Lucy's 'Tui Street Princess' had tiny pictures of fruit cut from yoghurt containers glued onto her dress. Terri's 'Soccer Ball' was her favourite though. Terri had flattened drink cans and arranged them into alternating squares of colour to make a soccer ball. Beside it, was a soccer boot made out of used cardboard, with real boot laces threaded through it.

Ella gazed at Terri's artwork while listening to Serena chatting with other parents. Ella's dad was with Serena. He'd just arrived from work. He stood tall as the tree in front of Jack's house, nodding and occasionally contributing to the conversation in his deep, low voice. Funny how his spoken voice was so different from his laugh. When he laughed, the sound was lighter, as if floating towards the clouds. Towards heaven? For a moment, Ella's stomach felt empty. Her mum wasn't here to see her own portrait.

"I love this 'Soccer Ball' piece." Serena's voice interrupted Ella's thoughts. Her hand was on Ella's arm. Her bangles tingled and her perfume almost shimmered around Ella's face, until she had no choice but to breathe it in deeply.

"You smell nice," Ella said, surprised she hadn't noticed that before.

"Thanks." Serena's hand was still on Ella's arm and for the first time ever, Ella didn't feel the urge to nudge it away.

"This is my favourite," Ella said.

"Is it? Very clever use of materials – and I like the colours she's used."

"Is it your favourite too?" Ella asked, twisting a

strand of her brown hair around her finger. Her hair never stayed in a ponytail properly.

"I like it a lot, but it's not my favourite."

"Which one is then?"

"Yours, Ella," Serena said, turning to look at Ella. "I love the way you've created an image of your mother with such care and attention. I think it's a beautiful portrait."

Ella's hair was so tightly wound around her finger that it hurt. She unwound it slowly. Serena's hand was still on her arm. Ella looked at it. Serena followed Ella's eyes, gave her arm a little squeeze then let go.

"Shall we show your dad your portrait?" Serena asked. "He hasn't had a chance to see it yet."

Ella nodded and followed Serena and her jingling bangles over to her father.

Interrupting a discussion between Ella's dad and some other parents, Serena took him by the elbow. "Excuse me, everyone," she said. "I'm just going to steal Bob away for a minute to show him his daughter's art work."

"Yes, of course, that's what I've come to see," Ella's father agreed. Turning away, he looked around him. "Where is Ella?"

"She's right here." Serena reached behind her and

gently pulled Ella to her side.

"Ah, there you are." Ella's dad put his hand on his hip. "Here, take my arm. It's only appropriate that the artist accompanies me. Lead the way."

Ella hooked her arm through her dad's and took a few steps, then stopped. "Dad, I think I should warn you that it's a—"

"Portrait of Mum. I know. Serena told me. She said it's very good. Come on. We'll have a look, shall we?"

In front of the portrait, Ella and her dad looked like any other father and daughter at an exhibition. No one could have known how much every tiny component of the portrait before them mattered, how every little part of the face had an importance of its own.

"You've got the colour of her hair exactly right," Ella's dad remarked.

"I hope so. There were lots of bits of material in a box and finally I thought that was the right colour, but then I couldn't remember if it was exactly right. Sometimes I forget things about how she looked."

"The colour is perfect, Ella. It must've taken you ages to cut it into those strips. It really looks like her hair."

Ella could hear Jack somewhere down the

other end of the hall. He was laughing loudly. She wondered what was so funny. Her dad turned to her. His eyes were watery. "You've even got the little freckles on her cheeks."

"Serena helped me with that. We picked up tiny bits of gravel on the concrete."

Ella's father nodded slowly. "I couldn't talk about her, Ella," he said quietly. "It's still hard for me. I didn't know how to help you. I could see you were so sad, but I—"

Ella interrupted, "I was okay, Dad."

"Sorry," he said quietly, "for how I was."

His big, warm hand wrapped around Ella's. She wasn't sure what to say to him, so she squeezed his hand instead.

Under the moon, Serena and Ella walked home from the exhibition. Ella's dad had driven the little girls home, but Serena and Ella had decided to walk. Behind them, Awatiu School was almost in complete darkness now, with just the faint glow of a few sensor lights. Ella's ponytail bobbed as she jumped slightly to avoid the cracks in the pavement. 'Step on a crack, marry a rat!' she thought. Sometimes she still played that game with herself.

Suddenly she stopped and turned to face Serena.

"I hate rats, Serena."

"I'm not that fond of them myself. Oh, and by the way, I have asked your dad to bury the water rats down the bottom of the garden in future. I don't think he really thought about how unpleasant that would be for you when you sorted the recycling. Shouldn't be many rats now though, since the council sent pest control to get rid of them," Serena said. "Also, we thought we'd try to put the recycling in a separate bin inside, so that you don't have to sort it all on Monday nights."

"Two bins inside? That's a good idea." Ella walked beside Serena. The evening had become cooler, but the sky was clear and the moon – a golden, smile-shaped crescent – lit up the path for them as they walked.

"I saw you, y'know." Ella spoke even as she wondered whether she should say anything. She reached nervously for a strand of hair.

"Saw me?"

"With those tiny people. I saw you."

"Ah."

Ella looked up at Serena. She hoped she wasn't annoyed. Serena's face was the colour of honey under the moonlight. She nodded gently.

"Does Dad know?"

"He knows."

"Jack thinks you're my fairy godmother."

"What do you think?"

"You might be."

Serena smiled.

A car passed and tooted its horn. Jack leant out of the window, waving and yelling, "'Night, Ella. We're gonna beat you home!"

As Ella waved at him, she noticed Serena doing her special wave, as if with a wand, as if to make wishes come true.

"Do you want to race me, Ella?" Serena asked. "Race you to the corner of Tui Street. Last one there marries a rat. Ready, set, go!"

Ella was so used to not joining in that for a moment she stood and watched Serena sprint away from her. She was surprisingly fast. Then it occurred to Ella that she'd better get moving or Serena would win. Within seconds she'd not only caught up with Serena, but was sprinting past her.

Up ahead, the Tui Street sign glinted in the moonlight. They were nearly home.

Harry and Gemma

GEMMA AND HARRY SAT in the peach tree in their mum's back garden, looking across to the next-door neighbour's. From high in the branches, they could hear the familiar clink of Jack's back door as he walked outside.

The twins lived in two homes. One was with their mum in a sunny, wooden house in Tui Street, where they had always lived before their parents separated. They would spend one week there with their mum, and the following week at an apartment across town with their dad and Lula, his new partner.

Their father liked the apartment because he didn't have to do any lawn-mowing or hedge-cutting or peach-tree pruning. He'd hated those jobs in Tui Street. The apartment had no trees. It was on the third floor of a shiny, silver building, with tinted windows that looked out onto a park. Their dad said that was how he liked nature: something he could look at, but didn't have to look after. He liked the neatness and tidiness of the apartment too. It was like Lula: clean and perfectly organised.

It was late on a Friday afternoon. Through the branches of the peach tree, it looked to the twins as if twigs were growing out of Jack's head – a human with antlers. Hearing their laughter, Jack looked up. "Hey!" he called. "You back for the whole week now?"

"Yep. Dad dropped us back after school," Gemma replied.

Climbing over the fence, Jack swung up to join them in the tree. "Better not've eaten all the good ones," he said, reaching for a large, juicy-looking peach. He bit into it and, slurping peach juice, asked, "Your new school good?"

Gemma and Harry had recently moved to a new

school called Visions, which was near their dad's apartment.

Harry shrugged his shoulders. "It's okay."

Jack swallowed a mouthful of peach and said, "Weird name, 'Visions'."

"Weird school too," Harry said.

"You have to call the teachers 'Sir' or 'Miss'," Gemma said, "and wear a hat and a tie. It's not like Awatiu. Lula thinks Visions is better, though."

Before they'd moved schools, Lula had sometimes picked Gemma and Harry up from school, so Jack knew what she looked like. She had short, blonde hair, flattened against her head, and always wore red lipstick. Her real name was Louise, but she preferred to be called Lula.

"I bet you don't miss our assemblies," Jack said. "It was an hour long today. I got such a numb bum! Why don't teachers let us sit on cushions?"

Gemma and Harry laughed.

A voice came from the open window in Jack's kitchen. "Jack, instead of talking about your numb bottom, do you think you could pick a lemon like I asked you to?"

"Sorry, Mum. In a minute." He whispered to the twins, "She's like that guy from X-Men – Professor X. No matter where I am, she knows what I'm saying.

Probably reads my thoughts!"

"She'd be Phoenix then, cos she's a girl," Gemma said. "I'd love to have telepathic powers. Like when Lula talks about Mum, I'd love to know what she's thinking."

"Mean stuff," Harry said. "Lula doesn't like Mum."

"Why?" Jack asked.

Harry scratched his head. "Dunno. She just says mean things about her."

"Like when I got my new dress," Gemma explained. "She said, 'Did your mother choose that?' I told her I chose it but Mum paid for it. Then she said 'I suppose it's nice.' I suppose!"

"And like she told us that Visions School would be better for us," Harry added, "but then we heard her tell her friend that now Dad wouldn't have to run into Mum any more when he takes us to school."

Jack nodded. Gemma and Harry's mum was a gardener who worked part-time at Awatiu School and part-time for the secondary school close by.

"Lula's like my new teacher. They both love rules," Harry said. "Mr Springview says I have to cut my hair, even though it's tied up like the girls' hair – so I shouldn't have to cut it."

"He made him pick up rubbish yesterday for not getting it cut," Gemma added.

"Mr Tāmati would never do that," Jack said.

"Wish we could come back to Awatiu." Harry reached up and pulled his hair tie out, releasing a headful of black ringlets that reached halfway down his neck. "Know what? I might come back. Never wanted to go to that stupid school with dumb hats and ties anyway."

"We can't just leave," Gemma said.

"You don't have to, but I will," Harry said. "If he says anything else about my hair, I will."

"Jack, kai time," Jack's mother called through the kitchen window. "And please bring me that lemon!"

"I'd better go," Jack said, "but after dinner, everyone's playing soccer. Tim, Terri, Lucy, Ella, they'll all be there. See ya then? "

"Yep," Harry said. "See ya then."

"I'll bring my skateboard," Gemma said.

Jack scrambled down the tree and began to climb over the fence between their houses.

"Jack, did you hear me?" his mother called.

"Coming!" Jack replied. Under his breath, he added, "Professor X." He jumped off the fence, yanked a lemon from the tree and disappeared from sight.

"Phoenix!" Gemma called after him. "Your mum's a girl!"

That night Harry had a dream that they were at the apartment. Lula was in the kitchen, timing everything she cooked precisely, so that beeping sounds were going off every few minutes. Suddenly Harry realised that the beeping wasn't coming from the oven or the microwave, but from inside Lula's head. When he looked carefully at her short, blonde, gelled-flat hair, he could see a faint hint of wires, screws and bolts underneath her scalp. Now Harry knew why she was so neat and fussy; she was a robot.

Harry woke up, hot and sweaty, and went into his mother's room. Once it had been his parents' room, but now she slept there alone. He climbed in beside her.

"You okay, Harry?" she asked sleepily, reaching out and stroking his head.

"Had a bad dream."

"Want to tell me about it?"

"Nah," Harry whispered.

"Just wake me up if you change your mind." His mum put her hand over his and, within seconds, her breathing slowed and Harry knew she was asleep.

Harry lay awake for a long time. Here, he could climb in his mum's bed if he had a nightmare. He could help himself to food from the fridge. At the apartment, they only ate the food that Lula put on the bench for them to eat. Here they played soccer and skateboarded. At the apartment, Lula told them there were to be no soccer balls or skateboards inside, in case things got broken.

Harry and Gemma knew that Lula only tolerated them when they were there because she knew their father wanted them. If she made her feelings clear to their dad, she might lose him. Surely he would realise that? If Harry or Gemma had to run back down the hallway to put their shoes on or grab their raincoat before they went out, she would jingle her keys impatiently and roll her eyes. She even did their washing separately, as if they had germs she might catch. Lula cleaned every day. She sprayed citrus air freshener around the apartment so often that she herself smelt of antiseptic and lemon. Once, she took some crystal glasses from the top of the kitchen shelves to polish them. "Don't touch!" she'd said, when Harry reached over to pick one up. The twins had watched as she wiped the glasses over and over, until they gleamed so brightly that they hurt their eyes.

Eventually, Harry began to drop off to sleep but, as his eyelids closed, the memory of Lula's face when he'd dropped a glass of milk on the coffee table came into his mind. Thankfully, the glass hadn't broken, but the milk had seeped into Lula's magazines. Her lips had tightened around her teeth, stretching wide and white. As her eyes narrowed, he heard her cell phone, sitting on the table away from the spilt milk, making a strange sound, as if a hoarse, cackling woman was on speakerphone. Over this croaky laughter, Lula spoke in quiet, clipped words. "Harry, obviously you're not sensible enough to carry a drink into the lounge. From now on you can drink at the kitchen bench or sit at the table. No food or drink in the lounge again for either of you."

The next morning, Terri, Ella, Tim, Jack and Lucy were at the door with a soccer ball.

"Four versus three, like last night," Terri said to them. "Better than three versus two when you're at your Dad's." Terri was such a good player that the team she was in always played with one less player. Even then, the team Terri was in always won.

Gemma stood up, pushing her plate away. "Mum, please can we do the dishes when we get back?"

Their mother nodded and smiled, saying, "Oh, all right. After a week away from your friends, I suppose the dishes can wait."

The seven friends charged down the hallway and out the front door, where Tui Street waited in the

Saturday morning sun, a wide, friendly cul-de-sac waiting for players.

The following Friday, the twins' mother nosed the car into the traffic on the main road off Tui Street. Gemma and Harry were snuggled up in the crocheted rugs their mum kept in the car. In the early morning like this, when the other Tui Street kids were probably still asleep or just waking, the rugs helped them feel that they too were still curled up in bed.

Their mother turned the radio to their favourite station. The car bounced over the speed bumps that their dad always said she took too fast. At the lights, she turned to Gemma in the front. "You've got the mobile phone, haven't you?"

"No, Harry's got it. You gave it to him."

"Yeah, I've got it."

"Oh, that's right. I remember," her mum said, tapping her fingers on the steering wheel.

The school was much closer to Dad and Lula's apartment than their home in Tui Street. When they walked from Dad's, it took ten minutes, but from Tui Street, because of the busy roads in between, it was forty minutes' drive. The motorway was the worst bit, with endless queues of cars that moved like snails.

Finally, they turned off a busy street, into a quieter, no-exit street, with trimmed trees on neatly-mown grass verges. From here, the twins could see a tall, bold, silver sign that said, 'VISIONS – looking to the future'. A shiny metal gate opened automatically as the car approached. Inside, the car followed the wide, curved driveway with neatly arranged gardens on either side. Tall, gleaming buildings towered up ahead. Children in wide hats, ties and long socks made their way through sliding doors into the buildings.

"We're here," Gemma and Harry's mum said. She parked the car in a space marked 'Visitor' then looked at the children in the rear-vision mirror. "Don't forget both bags. I've washed all the clothes that belong at Dad's place, so put them in your drawers there. Maybe leave the clothes bag in the school office for today, so you don't have to carry it around with you." She reached over and squeezed Harry's shoulder. "And hey, your hair looks very tidy, Harry. I'm obviously the best bun-woman in New Zealand! Give me hair that mustn't touch a collar and I can whip that hair into the tidiest, off-the-collar bun you've ever seen!"

She was trying to cheer them up. Gemma forced a small smile from her lips.

Harry didn't bother. "Wish you'd just left us at our old school with our friends."

Their mother nodded. "I know you do. I'm sorry. I didn't have the energy to keep battling Dad and Lula over schools." She stepped out of the driver's door to hug them. "Come on, you'll be late. You sure the mobile phone's in your bag, Harry?"

Harry nodded.

"Good. Text or phone any time you like. I'll always answer." Their mum leant down and kissed them both on the cheek. "Just reach up and touch your cheek, whenever you need a kiss. It will be there until you come home."

Harry and Gemma nodded, mumbling their goodbyes quietly. Harry was bigger than Gemma and could carry his clothing bag. Gemma had to click the wheels out at the bottom of her bag and drag it behind her. It rattled noisily over white pebbles cemented neatly into the driveway. She could still feel Mum's kiss on her cheek and smell the hint of strawberry from the lip balm her mother wore. Her hand tightened on the bag handle. It was too early to start missing her mum. She'd only just said goodbye.

Mr Springview was standing at the door of his classroom when Harry arrived. He wore a grey suit, with a gold tie, and had sunglasses perched on his head above his tanned, neatly-shaven face. Harry thought he looked like the men in TV ads who wore suits and drove fast cars. Above him, little security cameras blinked. They and Mr Springview watched Harry hang up his bag in the corridor outside the classroom. "Morning, Harry," he said.

"Morning, sir." Harry took out his homework and walked towards the door.

"Hats off in the classroom, young man," Mr Springview said. "You should know that by now."

Harry stopped. His shoe squeaked on the polished floor. He turned back to the line of gleaming, new, steel hooks where his bag was hanging. He took off his hat and hung it on the hook. He knew Mr Springview was looking at his hair, which his mum had neatly twisted into a bun.

"I see you still haven't had your hair cut, Harry," Mr Springview said. "Do you enjoy picking up rubbish?"

"Sir, my mum told me as long as it's pinned up so it doesn't touch my collar, it's okay. The school rules say it mustn't touch our collars."

"That rule is for girls, though. Until you cut your hair, young man, you'll be doing rubbish pick-up every lunch time." Mr Springview turned and walked into the classroom where he stood behind his desk, staring at his laptop screen.

Harry stood in the corridor, biting his lip. He didn't want to go in. He could see the bright, white walls and steel-framed desks set out in straight lines. He thought of Mr Tāmati's welcoming room, with cushions in the corners, and books, packs of cards and Lego on the shelves.

Without looking at Harry, Mr Springview called, "Come on, Harry, school's about to start."

The other kids in the classroom looked up at Harry when he entered. He knew his face was red. He wished he could loosen his tie, he felt so hot. With a slow breath, he pushed his feet forward, one after the other, and made his way into the classroom to his desk.

Ten minutes after the morning-tea bell, Gemma finally found Harry. He was sitting in a doorway on the cold concrete, his school bag on his lap.

"There you are," she said. "I've been looking for you."

Harry looked up. "I want to get out of here," he said.

"Harry, we—"

"I hate it here." Harry looked down at his fingers.

Gemma nodded. She could see Harry's fingers curling and uncurling on his lap.

"Wish Mr Tāmati was still my teacher," Harry said.

Gemma nodded again. "Me too."

"Then let's just go."

"Back to Awatiu?"

Harry nodded. "We'd see Mum. She's working there today."

"We don't know which bus to catch."

"We could walk."

"Walk!" Gemma rolled her eyes.

"We might get there by the end of school. We could say hello to Mr Tāmati."

Gemma looked away. Soon the strange buzzer would go to signal the end of morning tea. "I think I know how to get to the motorway," she said. She looked down at her brother. He was usually the less confident one, the one who had nightmares and chewed at his lip when things felt difficult. Since they'd come to Visions she'd noticed a change in him, as if his hurt and anger were making him stronger.

"Come on. Let's go," she said. Reaching down, she pulled him up. "We need to get our schoolbags first," she said. "Not our clothes bags. We'd be noticed. Too heavy, anyway." Gemma turned away and began to walk determinedly, her long, dark plaits barely moving, they were pinned so firmly under her hat.

Nobody stopped them as they made their way out of the wide driveway. A teacher passed them in her car, giving them a small, uncertain wave, but she kept going.

At the top of the driveway, the shiny, metal gate opened as they walked towards it. Two security cameras were perched on top of the pillars at either side of the gateway. They swivelled from left to right, as if endlessly searching. Harry looked at their empty glass eyes. "They're probably watching us in the school office," he said.

Gemma looked down, so the camera couldn't see her face. "Come on. We'd better walk faster."

They walked out onto the street and past the neat, bright white and silver houses positioned in the exact middle of each plot of land. Some houses hid behind huge front gates that were twice the height of the twins. Beside them were keypads with secret codes that only the owners knew. Other houses had security cameras that simply gazed and observed, hour after hour.

"Nothing's normal here," Harry said.

Gemma nodded. "So clean," she said. "And tidy."

"Like Dad's apartment," Harry said.

They turned onto the busier road, where Mum had driven them earlier. It was noisy and both children were quiet as traffic sounds swirled around them.

People were rushing, walking quickly, speaking on mobile phones, slamming car doors and getting on and off buses as if there were urgent things they had to do. Most people wore suits, like Lula, whose skirts matched her jackets and high-heeled shoes. Harry thought of his mum with her gardening gloves and gumboots and a lonely part of his stomach began to ache.

"How far do we go on this road?" Harry asked.

"There's a motorway sign somewhere, I think."

"What colour is it? What does it say?"

"It's blue. Don't know what it says. Maybe just 'south' or something." Gemma walked a little further, then stopped. "Hey, use the GPS on our phone, Harry. That'll show us the way."

Harry nodded. "Okay." He took out the phone and keyed in 'Tui Street, Awatiu'. A map appeared with a blue line pointing ahead. They were going in the right direction. Harry looked up. Hopefully they'd see a blue motorway sign soon. If Jack were here he'd want to hold the phone to track their movements on the GPS. He liked maps, charts and facts. Harry thought of Jack and Tim, playing soccer or skateboarding at school. Terri would be with them and Louie, the new boy, from the top of Tui Street. Ella and Lucy would be on the flying fox or the obstacle course. If he and Gemma could just find a blue motorway sign, they could join them all soon.

It was hot and sticky, so the rain was a relief when it came, although their hats began to droop. Harry took his off, squeezed the water out of it and shoved it in a side pocket of his backpack.

"It'll get ruined squashed up like that, Harry." Gemma took hers off and shook it a few times.

"Who cares," Harry declared. "I'm not going back to that school anyway."

"Did you get in trouble this morning?"

Harry shrugged.

Gemma stuffed her wet hat back on her head, dislodging her pinned-up plaits in the process. "What if they make us go back?"

"I'll keep leaving," Harry said. "I'll just keep on walking home." The phone in his hand made two small beeps. Someone was texting them. "It's Mum." He pressed the button to open the text and immediately a hoarse cackling coughed from the phone. Harry dropped the phone.

"Harry!" Gemma yelled. "You'll break it!"

Harry stepped backwards. "It's that horrible laughing," he yelled back. "From Lula's phone!" It was the same sound Lula's phone had made the day he'd spilt the milk.

Gemma picked the phone up. She closed the text. The taunting laughter stopped.

"She's hacked our phone, Gem." Harry said. He felt sticky and hot. He pulled his water bottle out of his bag and drank from it. "We need to keep walking," he said.

Half an hour later, the blue motorway sign still hadn't appeared. The rain had stopped and steam rose from the roads and footpaths.

"The motorway isn't as close as I thought it was," Gemma said. "It seemed so quick to get to here in the car." She stopped. "I need to eat my apple, Harry. I'm hungry." She sat on a brick wall outside a house and unzipped her backpack. Behind her, she felt as if something was watching them. Turning, she saw a security camera blinking methodically. Another camera seemed to be facing that camera. Did they watch each other? Did the cameras themselves check that other security cameras were behaving?

"Do you think this GPS is working?" Harry said, sitting beside her.

"Hope so." Gemma frowned against the glare of the sun. Up ahead, she thought she could make out signs in the distance. She stood up, bit into her apple and began to walk again. "Actually, I think I can see the sign."

They walked past a supermarket with gleaming trolleys, a kindergarten where a single child climbed a tree, a dog sitting obediently outside a library, the empty train station, and shops with brand new things stacked efficiently in their windows.

"There it is!" Gemma said, pointing to the blue sign ahead. "Motorway south."

Harry looked up. "Motorway south," he repeated. The blue arrow on the GPS was pointing to the motorway, while a British woman's voice told them to take the second exit at the roundabout.

The on-ramp to the motorway was just up ahead. Harry recognised it now. This was the motorway their father drove them home on. Harry thought of how relieved he always felt when Dad drove them back to Tui Street, away from Lula and her fussy rules, away from her lowered eyelids and the whisper she used when she was saying something about them to their father.

"It doesn't have a footpath," Gemma said to Harry.

Harry kept walking.

"Harry!" Gemma yelled after him. "There's no footpath!"

"Course there isn't! It's a motorway!" Harry yelled back. "Thought you knew that!"

Gemma stopped walking. "It's too dangerous!" She watched Harry as he continued, keeping to the left of the motorway on-ramp.

Cars whizzed past Harry, too fast and loud for him to think properly. Their fumes rushed at him like bad breath.

"Harry!" Gemma screamed after him. "Come back! You'll get killed!"

A car tooted at him and somebody yelled, "Get off the motorway!"

Harry stopped. Behind him, at the start of the on-ramp, he could see Gemma. She looked small and was holding her hat on her head with both hands to stop the hot wind from blowing it away. He'd have to turn back. There had to be another way to get back to their mum, to Awatiu School. Visions, he thought, what a dumb name.

The familiar hoarse cackling sound came from the phone in his hand. This time he resisted the impulse to throw it down. It felt hot and prickly in his hand. A pink car slowed beside him, its roof down. Harry recognised it immediately. The car pulled in just ahead of him and Lula stepped out, her high heels clacking, as she walked towards Harry.

"You must go back to school, Harry," she said.

Harry shook his head slowly. The hoarse laughter crackled sharply in his hand.

"Go back to school," Lula repeated. "You're ruining everything. You need to behave, so your father can be happy with me, Harry. Don't you want your father to be happy?"

Harry didn't speak. His hand hurt.

"Are you listening, Harry?" Lula's eyes narrowed, her lips whitened as they stretched over her teeth.

Harry shook his head again. He wanted to walk back to Gemma.

"I watch you, Harry," Lula said, "both of you, all the time. See this?" She held out her own cell phone. The volume of the cackling doubled and Harry realised Lula's phone was laughing hoarsely too. The screen on her phone showed a large, wide-open eye. The eye began to stretch out of the phone as if pushing against clear plastic. Seconds later it burst through and flew at Harry, like a large, crazed mosquito. Whirling and swerving, it rushed at him over and over. Harry batted it away, ducking and dipping, until Lula, delighted at the chase, laughed raucously herself. Then Lula clapped her hands and the eye flew back immediately, dissolving into her phone screen again. With four efficient taps, Lula keyed a code into her phone and the dry, empty cackling stopped.

"See, Harry? I've got my eye on both of you," she said. "No point trying to get Mummy to take you home. She can't text you and you can't text her. So get back to school and behave." Lula turned, put the cell phone in her suit jacket pocket and climbed back into her car. Without looking back, she sped off into the distance until she was just a pink spot on the motorway.

Harry began to walk back to Gemma. They had to get off this motorway. Even more importantly, they had to get away from Lula and Visions.

Gemma walked towards him. "Who was that? Was it Lula?"

Harry nodded.

"What did she say?"

"That we have to go back to Visions and stop ruining things."

"Ruining things? Us?" Gemma shook her head. "*She's* ruined things! So has Dad."

"She did this weird thing. An eye came out of her phone," Harry said. He swallowed uncomfortably.

"It chased me."

"An eye?"

"Yeah and her phone laughed again ... like a witch. So did ours. She's definitely hacked it so Mum can't reach us and we can't reach her."

"Can we text anyone else?"

"Dunno. Don't want to try."

Gemma looked at Harry. His face was pale and his lip twitched nervously.

"Maybe we could get the train," Gemma said.

"It doesn't go to our station. Remember? Mum checked to see if we could get the train to Visions when we first started. It goes into town and then you have to swap trains."

"We could do that," Gemma said. "We could swap trains in town."

Harry stopped beside her. "Got any money?"

"Two dollars."

"I've got five. That might be enough."

They turned from the noisy motorway and walked back the way they had come. Back over the busy road, back past the shops, until they reached the train station.

When the teachers at Visions School phoned the twins' parents to tell them their children had disappeared, both parents immediately texted and phoned the mobile in Harry's bag. Why hadn't he answered? Lula told their father to call the police, even though their mother had asked him not to just yet. Their mum was working in the gardens of Awatiu school and she walked over to her children's old classroom. Unlike Visions, with its rule that twins had to be separated, her children had been in the same class here.

Mr Tāmati was sitting at his desk. One of the pupils stood beside him, showing him something in her book. He looked up when the twins' mother knocked on the door. The Tui Street children smiled at her and waved. She gave a little wave, but she didn't smile. Mr Tāmati stood up and walked over to her. He spoke to her for a few minutes then opened the classroom door, asking Jack, Tim, Ella, Lucy, Terri and Louie to come outside.

Mr Tāmati spoke quietly to them, his eyes flicking from one child to the other. "Have any of you heard from Gemma and Harry today?"

The friends shook their heads.

"Do you have an idea of where they might be?"

"At that other school – Visions?" Jack suggested.

"They're not at school. Seems they were there this morning, but they've left," Mr Tāmati said.

"I've tried phoning and texting them," the twins' mum said. "I can't seem to get through." She sniffed and pulled out a scrunched-up tissue to pat her eyes.

Tim nudged Jack. Jack looked at him uncertainly. Tim's eyes widened, as if trying to relay his thoughts through his eyes.

"Jack, do you have something to say?" Mr Tāmati asked. "This is very serious, and if you have any information that might help us find them, you need to say it now."

"They could've been kidnapped," Lucy said.

"Lucy, don't be silly," Ella said. This was not the time for Lucy's imagination.

"Kids do sometimes get kidnapped, Ella!"

Mr Tāmati looked firmly at Jack. "Is there something you have to say, Jack?"

"Tell them, Jack. Tell them what you told me," Tim said quietly. He couldn't bear to see the twins' mother looking so frightened.

"Harry doesn't like his teacher, Mr Springview," Jack said. "He wants Harry to cut his hair and makes him pick up rubbish."

"And?" Mr Tāmati urged. "Anything else?"

Tim answered, "Harry said he was gonna leave school and walk home if Mr Springview told him off about his hair again."

"Walk home?" The twins' mother spoke for the first time. "To Tui Street?"

"Yep," Jack answered. "They hate Lula – and that school."

Gemma and Harry's mum took her cell phone out of her jeans pocket. Her fingers shook slightly as she tapped on it. "I'd better let their father know. Thanks, boys."

"Okay, back into class, kids," Mr Tāmati said.

From inside the classroom, Jack and Tim could see Mr Tāmati listening as the twins' mother spoke to their father on the phone. They saw Mr Tāmati reach out and put his hand on her arm.

Back in his seat, Jack leant over to whisper to Tim. "What if birds eat their crumbs?"

"It's not a fairy tale, Jack."

"Facts, Timbo, facts. Firstly, there's a brother and sister. Secondly, a wicked stepmother, and now the kids are trying to get back home."

Tim looked out the window at Mr Tāmati and the twins' mum. "Isn't there some witch in the story who tries to eat them?"

Mr Tāmati came back into the classroom. "Right, everyone. Titiro ki ngā pukapuka. Look at your books, please. Back to work."

There were stairs leading down to the station platforms. Each platform had a sign with train times and locations that flickered up and down. The train that went into the city was due to leave in three minutes. The station was empty. An old train ticket blew across the tracks in the warm wind. Gemma and Harry's rubbery footsteps jarred on the platform as they ran. Quickly, they slotted their coins into the ticket machine, while their train sat humming quietly. The children climbed aboard and sat down while the doors slid shut behind them.

An elderly man sat up the front of the carriage and a young woman sat in the middle by the window, listening to her iPod and singing softly to herself, with her eyes closed. She had spiky blonde hair with purple streaks in it. Gemma thought of Lula with her flat, blonde hair. Lula would never have purple streaks.

The train lurched forward. Harry rested his head against the window. The chugging vibration of the train was comforting. He smiled to himself. No more Visions. He reached up and pulled his hair from the neat little bun his mother had so carefully pinned up that morning. Ringlets of black hair fell around his neck and face. He reached into his bag to drink from his water bottle.

Beside him, Gemma leant back on the seat. She closed her eyes, but the idea of an eye coming out of Lula's phone and following them, watching them, came into her mind. Quickly, she opened her eyes again.

The phone in Harry's bag rang. Harry didn't move. There was no cackling. The ring tone was the usual one. Did that mean the call wasn't from Mum or Lula?

The old man up the front turned to see where the sound was coming from. He stayed in that position looking at Harry and Gemma. "Why don't you answer your phone?" he asked.

"It's not important," Harry answered.

"It might be someone from home calling, checking you are safe."

"I'll ring them back later," Harry said.

"Everything okay? You two aren't in any trouble, are you?"

"No," Gemma said quickly. "We're just going home."

The old man coughed, stood up and carefully made his way from his seat to perch on the seat opposite the children. "Wish I was going home," he said. "My real home was India."

Gemma and Harry nodded politely.

"Don't think this train will take me to India," the old man said, chuckling. "Take a bit of home with you is my advice. You won't miss it so much if you bring some of it with you."

Gemma reached up and felt her cheek where her mother had kissed her, the little bit of home she had with her.

The elderly man continued. "I still use an old remedy from India for keeping the mouth and teeth clean. I slosh sesame oil around my mouth for twenty minutes every morning. Look at my teeth now!" He smiled widely. His teeth gleamed white at them. "And look at my tongue," he added, poking his tongue out. "It's perfectly clean. I have never been to a dentist in my life."

Gemma and Harry laughed. For a moment, they had both completely forgotten about the eye, Visions and Lula.

The train slowed down. The elderly man stood up. "This is my stop," he said. "Get home safely, children."

No one spoke to them for the rest of the journey.

The city station, where they had to change trains, sat amidst tall buildings that cast long shadows over it. The sun reached its sticky fingers between skyscrapers, momentarily touching the twins' faces as they made their way along the platform to find a train timetable.

"Platform three – stops at Awatiu," Gemma said.

"Leaves in five minutes," Harry said, looking up at the station clock. "We'd better hurry."

It was when they sat down and looked out the window of the train to Awatiu that they saw the police officer. She was stopping people and showing them a photo as she came down the stairs to platform three. People shook their heads and shrugged their shoulders in response.

"Harry," Gemma said. "She's looking for us."

Harry's mouth went dry. The train started up. He could feel the vibrations under his tongue. He looked at the policewoman. She was nodding her head and speaking into a radio phone. She looked up and her eyes locked onto Harry's. Her eyes shifted to Gemma. She lowered the phone.

"Get down!" Harry said, pulling Gemma to the floor.

The train began to move. Gemma could hear voices. Someone yelled. A whistle blew. The noise of the engine grew. The train surged forward, towards Awatiu.

Gemma and Harry stayed on the floor. They

heard the carriage doors open. It couldn't be the policewoman. The doors had shut the moment she saw them. Harry swallowed hard. He bit into his lower lip. He looked at Gemma. She had her finger over her lips so he wouldn't make a sound.

There were no footsteps; only the hum and clatter of the train. Then a soft pitter-pattering made its way down the aisle. Harry clenched his eyes together. He pushed himself as tightly as he could underneath the seat. The tiny footsteps came closer and stopped right beside them.

Gemma and Harry slowly opened their eyes. In the aisle, a plump bird stood before them. Its chest was white and its body a mixture of greens, like the sea.

"A kereru," Gemma gasped, "like the ones at our creek, a wood pigeon, Harry."

Harry edged out from under his seat. There was a small, string bag hanging around the kereru's neck. He reached over. The kereru didn't move. Gently, Harry slid the bag over its head.

Gemma crawled forward. The bird stood very still, watching as Harry opened the bag.

"What is it?" Gemma asked.

"There's a note." Harry pulled out a carefully-folded piece of paper and passed it to Gemma. "Two little bars of chocolate too."

Gemma unfolded the note. The writing wasn't familiar. She read it in a loud whisper, "Gemma and Harry, your mum's at my house. She's worried. Lula has interfered with phone communication between you and your mother, so I will contact you from now on. Write 'Yes' on top of this note and send it back in the bag with Kereru so I know you're okay. He'll fly back to me. When I get it, I'll text you. Please answer my texts. Love, Jack's mum."

Quickly, Gemma scrabbled in her bag for her pencil case. In large blue letters, she wrote YES, placed the note in the string bag and gently slid it back over the kereru's head. Immediately, the kereru pitter-pattered back up to the carriage doors, which opened with a loud, wind-filled rush. Lifting its wings, the kereru flew out into the hot summer afternoon towards Tui Street.

Gemma and Harry stayed on the floor eating the chocolate bars.

"Check the texts, Harry. Jack's mum might be trying to contact us," Gemma said.

"I just don't want to read texts from Visions or Dad or—"

"Lula. I know, but we have to answer the ones from Jack's mother."

Harry skipped the first text from Visions and the

second from his father. The next text was from Lula, which, after three attempts, he realised couldn't be deleted. Then there was Jack's mum's text:

Come to my house. Dad, Lula and police r next door at yours. Don't come down Tui St. Go via back streets. U will have 2 climb over creek. Your mum and I will b waiting 4 u. x

Gemma looked at Harry. "Any more?"

"Nope." Harry's voice quivered, "All this is my fault, Gemma. I've upset everyone."

"It's not your fault. It's Dad's ..." Gemma said, "and Lula's. Quick, put the phone away. I think we're near Awatiu Station."

Harry slipped the phone back into his bag and was almost standing, when Gemma gasped. He immediately dropped to the floor again.

"Oh no!" Gemma whispered, peeping out the window from her seated position on the floor.

"What?" Harry lifted his head very slightly so that he could see too.

There was another police officer on the platform. He'd been to their school once to talk to their class about how to keep safe, so he was even more likely to recognise them. Harry could see the police car on the street outside the station. Groups of people on the platform were looking around nosily.

"We'll have to run down to the last carriage and get off there. No one's down that end," Gemma said.

"Okay," Harry agreed. "Then we need to sprint to that fence down the end of the platform. Can you get over that?" Gemma was shorter than Harry.

"I'll try," Gemma said, slinging her schoolbag over her shoulder. "Ready?"

Harry nodded.

Gemma stood up and began to run. At the end of the carriage, she grabbed the door, yanked it open and fled through to the next carriage. Her bag slapped against her as she ran. She could hear Harry's breathing behind her.

The train had slowed to a standstill. One more carriage to go. Just one more carriage. Gemma wrenched the handle of the door, but it didn't budge. "Harry, it's stuck!"

"Let me have a go!" Harry lunged at the handle, but it didn't move. "It's locked. We'll have to jump off here!"

"We can't do that. It's a huge gap – there's no step!" Gemma felt her heart flutter anxiously at the wide gap she'd have to leap to the platform. She had shorter legs than Harry.

"Jump, Gemma. Jump!" Harry turned and leapt from the train. "Now, Gem!" He held out his hand.

"Quick, he's seen us!"

Gemma gulped. Where would the police officer take them? Back to Visions and Lula? She took a deep breath and ran forward, leaping as far as she could. One foot landed on the platform and one slid off it, so that she fell hard on her knee. "Ow!" she cried, but she pushed herself up and ran as fast as she could, with Harry beside her.

It was only when they reached the fence that Gemma and Harry allowed themselves to look back. The police officer was running after them. He yelled, "Stop! It's okay, I just want to help!"

The phone in Harry's bag began to cackle.

Gemma looked at Harry. Neither of them spoke. They threw their bags over the fence and began to climb.

Landing in the long grass on the other side, the cackling grew louder. Out of the scrubby bush surrounding them, something rose and flew at them.

"The eye!" Harry yelled. "Run!"

There was no time to think about exactly where to go. If they turned left, they'd reach Awatiu shopping centre. Straight ahead would lead to the river that wound around the mountains to the sea. Instead, they turned right. Harry, with his longer legs, ran ahead and Gemma sprinted behind him. Sweaty and panting, the twins ran across the grassy fields until eventually they came to a small street.

"Has it gone?" Harry asked, looking around him.

"Can't see it." Gemma wiped sweat from her forehead. "Harry, we can't go down streets. The police will see us."

"What else can we do?" Harry said, stopping to catch his breath.

Gemma nodded. "We'll have to cut through people's places or whatever, just to stay off the roads."

"Okay." Harry took his backpack off. "I need some water."

"Me too."

It was when Gemma bent down to open her bag that Harry noticed it. "Gemma, take your hat off," he said.

"What?"

"Take your hat off. Quick. Just do it."

The eye was on the brim of her hat. As Gemma reached up, the eye hurled itself at Harry, knocking violently at his forehead, pulling away and flying at him again.

"Get away from me!" Harry yelled, swatting at it. "Get away!"

The phone began to cackle in Harry's bag.

90

Slinging her bag over her shoulder, Gemma yelled, "Run, Harry! This way!"

They climbed over and under fences and dipped around letterboxes and hedges, while the eye bashed at their ankles and heels. All the while, the British woman's voice on the GPS continued to direct them from Harry's backpack, saying "Now turn left," or "In one hundred metres, turn right."

Some houses had dogs that barked from inside, which wasn't so bad if they moved quickly, before owners came out to check. If dogs were already outside, Gemma and Harry had to run up driveways and along the street briefly, before dipping back into a dog-free yard.

Puffing and sweating, the twins noticed the roads around them seemed more familiar. The cackling had stopped. The eye too had disappeared.

"I think it's gone," Harry said.

Gemma nodded, too breathless to speak yet.

"She's still watching us though," Harry whispered. "She told me she would be."

"And phoning us."

Harry wiped his wet forehead on his sleeve and looked around him. "We're near school."

"Yeah. School's finished, though."

Harry took the phone out of his pack: 4:30 p.m.

The late afternoon sun gazed sweatily down on them. From behind a row of abandoned old flats, the twins watched a police car crawl down the street. A policeman was talking into a radio phone as he looked from side to side out of the windows. As soon as he was out of sight, Gemma and Harry took off, scrambling up and down fences at the bottom of people's back gardens until eventually they could see Tui Street Creek in the distance. The trees Jack's mother had planted on the other side of the creek looked strong and shady from under the flat, tired heat of the sun.

The GPS voice announced: "You are at your destination." Gemma and Harry smiled at each other.

"I'm hungry," Harry said.

"I could eat a horse," Gemma said. "Hey, Harry, pass me the phone."

When he handed it over she turned off the GPS and texted Jack's mother:

We're at the creek, at the back of your house.

As they scrambled over the sludgy creek bed, the twins were relieved to see their mum running through the trees in Jack's back garden. "Thank goodness you're okay," she said, scooping them into her arms. She kissed the tops of their heads and rubbed their dirt-smeared cheeks. "Thank goodness," she said again, arms around them, as they walked back through the trees towards Jack's back door.

Jack's mum hugged them too. She made them hot chocolate and toasted cheese sandwiches and bathed and bandaged Gemma's bloody knee. "Tim's outside with Jack and Aroha," she said. "They're desperate to see you, but I told them to wait till a bit later. I think your father wants to see you both first."

Through the window, they could see their dad walking down the pathway to the front door. Jack's mother let him in. "I'll be outside with the kids if you need me," she said. "Need to pull some weeds out of the garden."

Their father hugged them both, then, wiping a tear from his eye, he sat down at the opposite end of the table from the twins' mother. "I asked the police to give us a few minutes," he said. "We need to talk." He looked at Harry and Gemma. He didn't look properly at their mum; he hadn't looked at her properly for a long time.

"Lula's not normal, Dad," Harry said. "She's got this eye thing that watches us."

"It chased us," Gemma added. "She hates us."

"Don't be silly," their father replied. "She's very fond of both of you."

"She's not, Dad, she—"

"Give it time, Harry," their dad interrupted. "You'll get to like her eventually."

"The kids want to come back to Awatiu School," their mother said.

"I gathered that," their father replied. "Why, guys? Visions is such a good school."

"They want me to cut my hair," Harry said.

"They make him pick up rubbish," Gemma added.

"Everything feels ... strange there."

"It's very flash – and they have all the latest technology," their father said.

"I don't like flash schools," Harry said. He sucked his lip in and clamped his teeth on it – but it was swollen and bruised and hurt too much so he let it go. "I want to go back to our old school and our old friends."

"What if I say no?" their dad asked.

"What if I say yes?" their mum responded.

Their father looked straight at their mother for a moment. Then he turned back to the kids. "So, if you go back to your old school, I'll have to drive you across town every morning and afternoon again."

Gemma stood up. Her knee was aching. She straightened and bent her leg as she spoke. "You could move closer, Dad. *You're* the one who decided to move away from here."

"Lula's happy in the apartment," their father said. "I am too."

No one spoke for a moment. The clock on Jack's kitchen wall ticked loudly. Outside, the warm wind rustled through the trees.

"I don't like Lula," Harry said quietly. His fingers tapped the table. "I don't want to stay in the apartment with her again ... ever."

"Give it time," their father said.

"Dad, we don't want to stay with you and her anymore," Gemma said. "Lula doesn't want us there anyway."

"I'll miss you though," their father said. He wiped another tear from his eye.

"Then move closer," Harry said. "You can visit us lots then."

Their dad didn't say anything. He liked the apartment.

"You can come and see us whenever you want," Harry said. "You can take us to the movies!"

"Or play tennis with us on the school courts in the evenings, like we used to," Gemma suggested. "Just don't bring Lula."

"Lula will feel left out," their father said.

Their mum stood up. "Well, that's not the kids'

problem – or mine," she said, picking up the cups and plates and putting them on the bench. "Now, I believe the police are waiting to talk to us."

Outside, a police car was parked in Gemma and Harry's driveway next door. Tim and Jack were up in the tall tree. They jumped down, eagerly running to join their friends.

"You okay?" Jack asked.

"Yep," Harry answered, "and we're coming back to Awatiu School."

"We're staying here from now on," Gemma added.

Jack put his arm around Harry's shoulder. "We were a bit worried, eh Timbo?"

"Yeah," Tim answered, "and Mr Tāmati kept phoning your mum all afternoon."

The police came out of the house next door and walked purposefully up the driveway to meet with the twins' parents. Behind them was Lula. She stared hard at Harry and Gemma; no expression on her face. Her eyes narrowed. A quiet cackle started from the phone in Gemma's pocket. A secret smile passed over Lula's face, her lip stretching white and thin across her teeth. She took her own phone out of her suit jacket pocket and held it out so that it faced the twins. From where they stood, they could see the eye pushing the screen outwards. Within seconds, the eye burst out and flew straight at them.

Gemma shrieked and ducked. Harry batted it away, yelling.

At that moment, a large kereru swept out of a kowhai tree by the fence. Swooping towards them, it snapped the eye up in its beak.

Lula let out a small scream. Smoke began to unfurl from her phone. Her hand shot up over her eye. The police turned back to look at her.

"No, no, I'm all right," she said. "Something in my eye."

The kereru swerved away, towards Jack's mother at her front door. The children turned and watched as it landed gently on the guttering above her.

The twins' parents had joined the two police officers. Lula stood apart from them, fiddling with her phone as wisps of smoke continued to rise from it, one hand still over her eye.

"We'd better go home," Harry said. "They probably want to talk to us."

"Tomorrow's gonna be pretty boring, after this," Tim said.

"We won't be bored," Gemma said, smiling. "I don't think I want another day like this, ever again!" She hooked her backpack over her shoulders and her damp hat fell to the grass by her feet.

"Eeww, you won't be wearing that anymore!" Harry said.

Gemma leant down and picked it up. Shaking it out, she quickly stuck it on top of Harry's ringlety head and said, "But it looks pretty good on you!"

"Eerrgh!" Harry tore the hat from his head and began to chase her. "I don't want your stinky old Visions hat!"

Jack and Tim watched them, grinning. "Hey," Jack called after them. "Don't forget, soccer after dinner!"

"It'll be four against three tonight," Tim said to Jack.

"And every night from now on, Timbo," Jack said. "The way it used to be."

Turning away, Jack and Tim saw Jack's mother looking up at the kereru perched on the guttering above her. Her lips were moving. The bird's head was tilted, as if leaning in to listen. Then, powerfully and slowly, its wings rose, green and wide like the sea, as it flew up and away, past the creek and into the distance.

Jack's mum looked at the children and smiled. "It's just a kereru," she said. "You've all seen one before!" She turned and went inside, leaving the door open behind her.

Waimoe

ELLA COULD HEAR TIM AND JACK from her house. "Are you guys in the tree?" she called. She had an idea she wanted to discuss with them.

Tim's head appeared through the branches. "Yip. Come over."

In a sunny patch of grass below Tim and Jack lay Edmund, an old Newfoundland dog.

Ella made her way across the road, a clipboard in one hand and a pen in the other. She looked like someone who had important things to do. Then she saw Edmund, and dropped onto the grass beside him, clipboard cast aside. She scooped as much of the big dog's body onto her lap as she possibly could. "Look who's here! It's Edmund." She buried her face in his neck. "Your grandma away again, Jack?"

"Yeah. Gone up north to visit friends."

"You're so lucky. You get to babysit Edmund." Ella's voice softened, as she stroked Edmund's sun-warmed fur. "I wish I could have you at my house, Edmund. Yes, I do. Yes, I do."

Jack peered down at her as she chatted to Edmund. The dog's tail thwacked on the grass as she cuddled and patted his long black fur. "He's too old," Jack said. "I wish he'd run and chase balls and sticks. He's boring."

"He is not! That's a terrible thing to say, especially when he loves you so much." Ella spoke to Edmund again, "You follow him everywhere, don't you, Edmund?" Giving him one last hug, she gently shifted him back onto the grass and stood up, clipboard back in hand. "Right, I need to talk to you two about the nature rescue project. Have you decided on your topics?"

"Nah," Tim answered. "I might do an endangered animal."

"I was thinking of Borneo," Jack added. "Dad and I watched a programme about it and people were trying to stop the forest from being cut down to plant palm oil trees."

"What's palm oil?" Tim asked.

"It's oil they get out of the palm trees, but orang-utans live in those forests and end up with nowhere to live. There were orphan orangutans whose mothers had starved. They looked sad, like humans."

"That's bad," Ella nodded. "I like orangutans."

"Yeah. Mum won't buy anything with palm oil in it now, but the worst thing is, Dad said they use it in chocolate!"

"Chocolate!" Tim's voice rose. "Why would they do that to chocolate?"

"I know," Jack agreed.

"Not all chocolate uses palm oil," said Ella. "Just read the ingredients on the packet." She clicked her pen and swept a straggle of brown hair behind her ear. "Anyway, back to the project." The boys turned to look at her. "I've got an idea for a group project for us three."

"All three of us together?" Tim asked.

"Yep, because we need both of your back yards for this project anyway."

"What for?" Jack asked.

"What's your idea?" Tim asked.

"We-e-e-ll ..." Ella said, her serious eyebrows lifting as she smiled, "my idea is that we rescue the creek. Instead of studying how *other* people are trying to rescue something, *we* could rescue something. The creek behind your houses is dirty and has rubbish stuck in it. We could clean out all the rubbish, and then ..." Ella lowered her voice and looked down behind Jack's house, as if she didn't want the creek to hear, "... this might seem impossible, but maybe we could try to turn it back into a real creek again, with water running through it properly." She looked at the two boys. "What do you think?"

Jack spoke first. "Hmmm. Well, it's different. No one else will be doing a project like that."

"True," Tim agreed. "They'll be using books and the Internet. We'll be doing an actual rescue."

"My mum knows something about that creek," Jack said. "She talks to it. She calls it 'Waimoe' – sleeping water. Once I asked her why it didn't have water running through it and she said it was an old story and it would take more than a human to fix that creek now anyway."

Jack shrugged his shoulders. Sometimes it was difficult to understand his mother.

"Sleeping water ... Waimoe," Ella repeated slowly, writing the words on her clipboard. "Anything else she said?"

"Not really, except that she plants trees in front of it cos she said the trees might help. I thought she meant the trees would make it shady, so the creek wouldn't stink so much in the summer." Jack swung down from the branch he was sitting on and landed with a small thud on the grass below. "But we could ask her. Come on."

Ella and Tim jumped down after him. They walked quickly, following Jack through his front door.

"Coming, Edmund?" Ella called behind her.

Edmund, old and slow, plodded into the house after them.

Jack's mum was out the back of the house trying to get the lawnmower started. His younger sister, Aroha, was dancing around in a purple tutu and gumboots. Just as Jack's mother was about to ask her not to dance quite so close to the lawnmower, she saw Jack and his friends coming toward them. "Guys, if it's food you want, you'll have to get it yourselves. I'm going to get these lawns mowed before I do anything else. *If* I can get the lawnmower to start!"

"We don't want food – we want to ask you something," Jack said.

"Okay, make it quick."

"You know our creek?"

"Yeah, Waimoe."

"We're doing a project on it. We need some information."

Jack's mother didn't answer.

"We're going to rescue it," Ella continued. "Get rid of all the rubbish …"

Jack's mum had turned away and was looking down at the creek through the trees. "Not sure it's a good idea for you kids to do your project on that creek. It's probably not very safe."

"Why? It's safe, Mum. There's hardly any water. Or do you mean the water rats? But the council got rid of most of them."

"I don't mean that, Jack. I mean that Waimoe has her own … history. Serious things. I'm not sure you guys should get involved with her, that's all."

The three friends looked at each other.

"You're making it sound dangerous, Mum. It's just a creek!"

Jack's mother looked at him for a moment. When she spoke again, her voice was quiet. "She's not just a creek."

The children didn't respond. Something uncertain fluttered between them.

Ella clicked her pen. "We'll be careful, if you tell us what to be careful of."

"We will," Tim added.

"Mum, what about if we get the lawnmower started, then we mow the lawns and then you tell us. That's a pretty good deal."

Jack's mother nodded slowly. "I guess it's time somebody helped her. She's been asleep a long time now. Most people have forgotten about her. Houses were built around her and she just lies there, unnoticed. I try to help her. I plant trees ... but they're not enough to wake her up. It's quite complicated." Jack's mum sighed. "Okay, you guys get the lawnmower going and mow the lawns. I'll explain about the creek later. Needs to be after dinner though. Has to be dark."

As Jack's mother walked back towards the house with Aroha, Ella wrote on her clipboard: 'Waimoe – sleeping water. Trees not enough to wake her up.'

She held her clipboard out for the others to see.

"Asleep for a long time," Jack said. "Like Sleeping Beauty."

Tim's eyes widened. "No, it's not a fairy tale," he said. "It's a nature rescue project. Why does it always have to be some fairy-tale thing, Jack?"

"Timbo, it is what it is." Jack reached down to start the lawnmower. "That's what Dad always says." Then, with one miraculous pull on the handle, the lawnmower coughed and grunted into life.

The darkness was beginning to slice through the trees with long swords of blackness. Tim had brought a torch, but when he took it out of his pocket, Jack's mum whispered loudly, "No torches, Tim. They won't come if there's any light."

Who were 'they', Tim wondered, and why was Jack's mum insisting they make no sound? It was almost impossible to be as quiet as she wanted them to be. Even their footsteps echoed in the evening air.

At night, the creek looked velvety dark. Anything could be lurking in its long, sloping body of slushy mud. Jack always thought that if the creek really were human, – a 'she' as his mother referred to it – it would be a skeleton that had sunk into the slimy earth with no muscles to get itself out. Everything about it seemed stuck. Even its inhabitants had become sluggish. During the day, Jack still saw the occasional rat waddle along the banks and slide lazily down to its hole. No other animals visited the creek now, apart from the occasional duck that quickly flew away when it realised the creek only offered a thin layer of grey, stagnant water.

"I think it might be best if we all sit here quietly, just slightly back from the edge," Jack's mum whispered. "The trees are the magnet for them. That's why I planted them, to make it the way it was long ago." Jack's mother lay back on the grass and looked up into the sky. The ground was damp. It was the beginning of autumn. Soon the earth would be wet, blending soggily with their trousers.

Ella lay down beside her, gazing at the stars, and whispered, "What was it like long ago?"

"It was all forest apparently and … hang on, Ella. Guys, listen. I think I hear something."

It was the faintest whirring, as if helicopters the size of fingernails were coming in their direction. Straining her eyes, Ella could make out tiny flickers of light moving through the air towards them. The closer they came, the louder their racing wings sounded. For a moment, Ella felt her breath stop still in her chest, as the tiny creatures crossed above them to the trees Jack's mum had planted. Silently, Ella rolled onto her stomach, her eyes tracking them carefully.

They seemed to be playing, dipping in and out of branches. When they swooped down low, it was easier to see what they looked like. Most had light reddish skin, although some were browner, like Jack's mum. Their hair was red-gold. They wore clothes made out of tiny pieces of flax. If Ella had scooped one up, it would have fitted in her hand.

Jack, his mother, Tim and Ella watched in silence. Some flew back over them and down to the creek, their light, glowing bodies tipping forward as if to drink from its water. Quickly they swooped back up from its banks, circling playfully, as they joined the rest of their group and made their way back off into the distance, away from Waimoe and the four secret onlookers.

Jack's mother sat up. "Let's go in. I'm getting cold."

"But, what were they, Mum? Who were they?" Jack was on his feet, brushing off his trousers.

"Let's talk about it inside." Jack's mum began to walk through the trees back to the house.

Inside the house, it was warm. Tim cupped his hands around his mug of hot chocolate. Jack slurped his off his teaspoon.

"Jack, drink it properly," his mum said. "It spills when you drink it like that."

"But it tastes better this way."

"It tastes the same, Jack – drink out of the cup," Ella said. "We've got more important things to talk about than your manners."

"Ka pai, Ella," Jack's mother agreed. "Okay. Just remember, I don't know much about them. All I know is they're called patupaiarehe – forest fairies. They have supernatural powers and only come out at night or in very foggy weather."

Tim looked at Jack and Ella. Surely they didn't believe this? There was no such thing as fairies.

"Patupaiarehe," Jack repeated.

"Forest fairies," Jack's mum said. "The land all around Tui Street was once forest that spread right up to the mountain behind your school."

"Why did they cut the forest down?" Ella asked.

Jack's mother shrugged. "All the usual reasons. People wanted farms and roads. Then the farms and roads spread and cities grew."

"So they cut more and more trees down?" Tim asked, trailing his tongue over the chocolate moustache on his lips.

"That's right – and the patupaiarehe had to find other forests to live in."

"But you told us it would be dangerous to do our nature rescue project on the creek, Mum. Those fairies didn't look dangerous to me."

"Jack, they are not a danger to you and your friends ... although, actually, some patupaiarehe are aggressive. Luckily, Waimoe's are very shy and gentle. One of the elders on the marae once told me that some patupaiarehe used to keep watch over humans, like guardians. These ones are like that."

"So what *is* the danger, then?" Ella asked quietly.

Jack's mother stopped for a moment and took a long drink from her cup, as if considering whether to say more.

"Come on, Mum. Tell us."

Jack's mother took a deep breath. "Well ... one of the big farmers in the area, Mr Thompson, wanted more water for his farm, so he built a dam, which stopped the stream water from moving in its normal direction. Instead, he diverted the water through some pipes to fill up a huge pond he'd dug on his farm."

"So that's why the creek's water became so low," Ella said, writing on her clipboard. "He made the water go into his pond."

"Well, yes, in the beginning that was why, but—" She stopped abruptly.

"Mum, keep going." Jack tapped his spoon on his cup impatiently.

"Stop that, Jack. Look, I don't know all the details, but someone smashed the dam down."

Tim looked at Jack, shaking his head. "So why doesn't the creek have water rushing through it again? It should be full of water now."

Ella looked down at her clipboard. She'd made notes during the conversation. "Okay, this is what I've got so far: Once there were forests and forest fairies, called patupaiarehe ... hope I've spelt that right."

"Just keep going," Jack said. "Mum can check later. I wanna hear the facts."

Ella continued to read from her clipboard. "Forests were cut down to build houses and farms." She looked up at Jack. "Like palm trees were for palm oil." Then she continued, "Forest fairies disappeared. A dam was built by Mr Thompson to get more water for his farm. Then the dam was smashed down."

Jack looked at his mother. "So, why is there hardly any water in the creek if the dam was smashed down? And who smashed it?"

"I'm not saying any more," Jack's mum said. "I don't think it's safe." She stood up, walked to the bench and began to rinse her cup in the sink.

"So, we're stuck," Tim muttered.

"There must be somebody who knows something though," Ella insisted quietly. "Some old person round here must remember things."

Jack's eyes widened. "Mum, what's the name of that old man who lives at the bottom of the street?"

Jack's mother came back to the table. "At the end of Tui Street?"

"Yeah."

"Mr Thompson."

"But that's the name of the farmer who built the dam. The one who started all the trouble. Wouldn't he be dead by now?"

"Yes, he is dead, but this is his grandson. This whole street used to be their farm. They sold all the farmland, but kept the house and the grandson still lives there. He's not friendly though. Never says hello. The dogs behind his fence look as though they'd eat anyone that came near them. You guys know the house we mean?" she said, looking at Tim and Ella.

They nodded. Any child in the street knew that house. There was a sign on the gate that said 'Beware of the Dogs', but in front of the word 'Dogs' someone had written the word 'killer' with red, dripping paint. Children never ventured near it at Halloween or to get sponsorship for a school walkathon.

"Bet he knows what happened after the dam was smashed down then," Jack said. "Let's go to his house and ask why the creek water never came back."

"That'd be good," Tim said. "Another interview. We'll get a good mark for this project."

Jack's mother looked at them. "Mr Thompson isn't a nice man," she said. "If you're going to interview him, you have to take Edmund with you."

Hearing his name, Edmund lifted his head momentarily and gazed expectantly at Jack's mother's face.

"Edmund?" Jack snorted. "He's too old to help us. What good's he gonna do?"

"Just take him. He might surprise you."

It was clear Mr Thompson did not want visitors. As well as the 'Beware of the Dogs' sign on his gate, another sign was attached to his letterbox that read 'No Trespassers'. Three dogs hurled themselves against the gate that kept them in the back yard. Although the dogs couldn't get to the front of the house, Tim, Jack and Ella stood hesitantly in front of Mr Thompson's property.

"All the curtains are closed," Ella observed.

"Maybe he's not home," said Jack.

"Who's going in first?" Tim asked.

Ella reached out and opened the gate. "I will. We've got a project to do." With her clipboard in hand, she unlatched the gate, stepped through and held it open for Jack, Tim and Edmund. "I don't mind doing the talking," she said, as she led the way down the path.

The doorbell didn't work, so Ella knocked three times. They waited. Nothing seemed to move within the house. The dogs continued to bark.

Ella looked down at Edmund sitting patiently on the step beside them. "He doesn't even bark back at them." She reached down to pat Edmund's wrinkled chocolate coat.

"I know," Jack agreed. "Granny trained him. He knows how to behave."

"No one's home," Tim said. "Shall we come back tomorrow?"

"Hang on. Shhh!" Ella leant backwards to see around the side of the house. "Someone's opening up the dogs' gate."

"The dogs' gate!" Jack's eyes widened. He turned and, jumping the three steps to the ground in one leap, began to sprint up the path to the front gate. Ella and Tim leapt after him, with Edmund struggling behind.

"Stop right there, before I let the dogs on you!" a voice boomed from behind them.

The three friends stopped and Edmund sank gratefully down into a seated position.

"Come back here. You don't go banging on an old man's door, then run off when he finally manages to get to you. Is that bad manners?" Silence. "Answer me!"

"It is," Ella answered.

"Yep," Tim agreed.

"We thought you were letting the dogs out," Jack explained.

"And why would I do that? Why would I let my dogs chase trespassers?" The old man's lips seemed to fall into a snarl, but whether he meant to look like that was hard to tell, because he had missing teeth, so perhaps his lips just had nothing to hold them in place. His face was wrinkled like a worn riverbed. "What do you want?"

"Are you Mr Thompson?" Ella asked.

"Who wants to know?"

"We need to ask Mr Thompson some questions."

"What about?"

"Just tell us if you're Mr Thompson first," Jack said.

"Bit cheeky, aren't ya?" Mr Thompson's snarl grew longer and wider. Maybe it wasn't the missing teeth after all.

"No, no. He's not cheeky. He's just, ah, he's just ..." Ella couldn't think with the old man glaring at her.

"In a hurry." Tim finished her sentence. "He needs to use the toilet." It wasn't the best thing to say, but he hadn't been able to think of any other reason for someone to feel rushed.

The old man's eyes moved back to Jack. His droopy lips lifted to speak. "There's a toilet inside."

"I can wait." If Jack had wanted to go to the toilet, he'd have preferred to go behind a tree than set foot in the old man's house.

"I am Mr Thompson. Now, what do you want to know?"

"We want to find out about the creek," Ella answered.

"The creek!" Mr Thompson's face turned pale. "Get off my property!"

The children began to turn away, but Ella stopped. She clicked her pen a few times and turned back. "We just want to know why it doesn't run like it used to."

"Do you now? Sorry to disappoint then." Mr Thompson turned away, reaching down to pat one of his dogs.

"You must know something!" Ella insisted.

Straightening up very slowly, Mr Thompson looked at Ella. His voice now was like a flat tyre, as if all the air had gone out of it. "Listen, girlie, maybe I do know something, but I'm an old man now. I don't want any trouble."

"Are you scared?" Jack asked.

Mr Thompson locked eyes with Jack, but it was like looking at someone on an Xbox: his eyes were there, but his thoughts had been sucked away somewhere else. "There's a lot to fear, boy. Even these dogs are terrified of it. Forget the creek."

"I'm not scared," Jack said.

"Me neither," Ella added.

Tim felt he had no choice but to join in. "Same," he said, but his heart was pounding as if it had moved into his ears. Surely the others were a little bit frightened?

"Aren't you now? Tell you what, eight o'clock tonight, you come back here. It only comes out at night. Once you've seen it, you'll keep your noses out of the creek." Mr Thompson turned away slowly. His head hung slightly forward as if he was walking into a strong wind.

Usually, Jack's parents let him do most things. He could play soccer with the Tui Street kids till after dark or skateboard at the local park for hours. He rode his bike all around Awatiu. This evening, however, Jack's parents had said he was absolutely not to go to Mr Thompson's house.

His dad had explained, "We don't mind if you go there during the day, but you stay away from there at night. Is that clear?"

"Why?" Jack had asked.

"Jack, just trust me," his mum had said. "It's not safe. You are not to go near his house at night. Got that?"

Jack had nodded, but he couldn't look his mother in the eyes. He had a feeling she'd see the truth if he did.

That evening, the Tui Street kids played soccer. They played four against three as usual, because Terri's team only needed three. She was as good as two players. She was so skilful and fast that Jack's dad reckoned she'd play for New Zealand one day.

When it became dark and everyone started heading home, Ella, Tim and Jack hung back.

"Dad thinks I'm going to your house, Jack," Tim said, "to work on our project."

"So does mine," Ella said, twisting her hair round her finger nervously. "I don't like lying."

"Me neither," said Jack. "My mum and dad think I'm going to your house, Tim."

"I don't want Dad not to trust me anymore," Tim said quietly.

"Look, this isn't just about the school project now; it's about the creek," Ella said. "We want that creek to have running water again, don't we?"

The boys nodded.

"So let's find out why the water never came back after the dam was smashed down. This is the only way. Hopefully, our parents will understand."

"Hopefully they'll never find out we did this," Jack said. "Come on, Edmund. You'd better come with us. If you go home without me, Mum'll be suspicious."

Mr Thompson's house looked even less inviting at night. There was a pale light coming from one of the rooms in the house; otherwise, it was completely dark. The pathway to the front door was difficult to navigate, as it snaked brokenly downward. Ella led the way, her breath puffing mistily in front of her, clipboard in hand. At her side was Edmund, tail wagging and panting softly.

Mr Thompson took a while to get to the door. When he finally did open it, amid the racket of dogs barking, his mouth fell into its toothless snarl. "Didn't think you'd come. Didn't think your parents would let you."

"'Course they did. Why wouldn't they?" Jack said, feeling a guilty twinge in his stomach.

"Hmmm. Well, come into the kitchen. You can see the creek from the window there." Mr Thompson led the children down an unlit hallway, past a lounge with an old, box-shaped TV silently flickering pictures. On a table beside it, one small lamp glinted weakly at them as they made their way to the kitchen.

In the darkness, Jack felt a surge of relief at the familiar objects on the kitchen bench: a kettle, a toaster, cups and a coffee jar.

"Don't be thinking I'm offering you anything to eat or drink," Mr Thompson said. "You're just here to look at the creek. You won't want to come back again after that. You won't care about water in the creek when you see what you're up against. Stand there – in front of the bench – so you can look out the window. It usually comes around now. Give or take a few minutes."

From the window, the children could see the bare land of Mr Thompson's back section curving down to the banks of the creek. It was starkly different to Jack's back yard, with its plants and the many trees his mum had planted.

Jack, Ella and Tim leant over the bench towards the window.

"Well, here we are," Ella commented.

"Yeah." Jack whistled softly through his teeth.

Tim reached down and patted Edmund. His fingers were trembling.

At the bottom of the empty, treeless lawn, something stirred. A shadow lifted from the depths of the creek and then, under the pale streak of moonlight, carried on up the creek bank, so that the whole back yard was swamped by its shape.

All three children took a step back from the bench. Mr Thompson, Jack noticed, had retreated to the back wall of the kitchen.

Jack realised he'd been holding his breath. With an effort from deep in his stomach, he forced the air out of his lungs as the shape advanced towards the house. "Whatever it is, it's massive," he whispered. "Or maybe it's just the shadow that's massive."

"Something's going on with Edmund," Ella said. Beside her, Edmund was growling.

"Shut your dog up. He'll bring attention to the house. I don't want that thing coming up here!" Mr Thompson stepped forward, as if to grab Edmund.

Quickly, Ella intercepted him and spoke gently to Edmund, who began to quieten and settle again.

The shape hadn't moved. Perhaps it had heard Edmund. Jack wished he hadn't had to bring that stupid old dog.

Holding Edmund's lead, Ella wiped her forehead. She was sweating. "Hey," she whispered. "I can see it now. Some kind of creature."

Tim peered through the window. "Definitely not as large as its shadow. See? Must be the moon behind it – made it look bigger."

Jack's eyes ached from the effort of trying to see the real shape of the creature in the darkness. "Some kind of massive ape thing."

As if aware that they were discussing him, the creature stood up straight, leant its head back and beat its chest with its fists. Wild-eyed, it lurched forward, circling the back yard. Its matted, rope-thick hair swung heavily as it thundered around the bare, hard earth.

Edmund began to growl again. He'd moved right up to the kitchen door, which opened straight onto the steps to the back yard.

"Shut that dog up or I swear I'll open that door and let him out to be eaten!" Mr Thompson's voice was thick with anger. He spat as he spoke.

Ella reached down to calm Edmund, but at that moment, the creature outside threw its head back, beating its chest again. If a sound were a knife, the sound it made could have cut through the very floor they stood on. It was sharp, desperate and filled with anger, like an animal in pain.

Ella stopped patting Edmund and concentrated on the sound. It reminded her of the crying sound her father had made after her mum had died: lost, sad and furious, all at the same time.

Edmund's growl erupted into a frenzy of barking and, yanking his lead from Ella's hand, he began to hurl himself at the kitchen door.

"That dog's gonna get us killed!" Mr Thompson lunged for the kitchen door handle. "If he wants to go out, let him out!" As soon as the door opened, Edmund was gone, quicker than Jack had ever seen him move.

"Edmund!" Jack ran to the door. Turning to Mr Thompson, he yelled, "What have you done? It'll kill him. It'll kill him! My gran loves that dog!"

Mr Thompson slammed the kitchen door shut. "You wanna go out there too? Listen boy, that dog was gonna make that gorilla thing come up here with all that barking."

Jack was shaking, furious tears in his eyes. He'd never dream of doing such a terrible thing to an animal. What kind of man was Mr Thompson? Who could let an animal run to its death like that?

Mr Thompson looked away from Jack and stepped back to the far wall.

Jack looked at Tim and Ella. "Edmund's too old," he said, his voice shaking. "He can't run fast. He'll get killed."

Tim and Ella both nodded, as speechless and helpless as Jack.

Out in the darkness, Edmund was visible. Through the window, they could see him walking steadily towards the huge creature. The wailing roar coming from its cavernous mouth slowly began to subside as it watched Edmund. The old dog walked further, closer and closer, until he was an arm's length from the creature. As if suddenly a little tired, Edmund sat down, facing it.

Slowly, the sound stopped altogether. Both creatures looked at each other.

"Mum's gonna kill me," Jack said. "That thing's gonna kill Edmund."

Tim reached over and put an arm around Jack's shoulders. "Edmund's okay so far. Look! Like Dad says, observe."

The ape-like creature threw its head back again and, tensing its whole body, wailed the most heart-breaking, anger-filled sound that ripped through the night like an ambulance siren.

Ella gasped. "Oh no, I thought he'd stopped that terrible sound. Poor Edmund. Don't bark at him."

Edmund made no sound. Instead, he continued to sit quietly, facing the creature that towered over him, piercing the night air with its sharp, wretched wails. As if letting a small child cry out the shock of a grazed knee, Edmund sat and listened. Eventually, the creature's voice weakened; the volume slowly leaked away. Its body seemed to flop, as if all the air had gone from it, and it stood, quiet and still, looking at Edmund.

The old dog seemed to be listening intently, even now, in this strange, unnerving silence. The creature continued to communicate soundlessly. It lifted its hands and wiped them over its forehead and eyes, as if tired. Its shoulders lifted in a shrug and fell again. Its head sank downward, chin on chest. Slowly, it turned away from Edmund and made its way back down to the creek, disappearing and taking its large, wide shadow with it.

Jack flung open the kitchen door. "Edmund! Here, boy! Come on, boy!" He stood at the top of the steps, arms stretched out.

Edmund stood up and slowly, carefully, made his way back to the top of the steps, wagging his tail. Jack knelt and pulled Edmund's warm, solid body in for a hug. He could feel his snuffly breath on his neck. "You are so brave, Edmund. So, so brave."

Turning to Ella and Tim, he said, "Let's go home. I want to get out of here."

Mr Thompson followed them silently to the front door. When Jack turned to say goodbye, Mr Thompson spoke first. "Never seen it do that. Never seen it go all quiet. Usually yells and cries and carries on, then just storms off down past the creek."

The children stood there quietly. It seemed Mr Thompson wanted to say more. "I just turn the TV up when I hear it and wait till it's gone. Can't stand the sound."

Tim looked through the lounge window at the lonely flickering of the TV set. "It must be hard for you listening to that every night. Do you get scared?"

Mr Thompson looked at Tim. His mouth opened, but he coughed instead. "My dogs get frightened," he said. "Anyway, visiting time is over. Go home." He turned away and shut the door abruptly behind him.

Into the still of Tui Street walked the three friends and the big, slow dog. It was hard to believe life had continued as normal outside Mr Thompson's gate. The moon still hovered gently behind the clouds, the streetlights lit up the same parts of the footpath and the houses had the same fruit trees, letterboxes and cars outside that they'd always had. None of those tucked away in their houses knew of the horror that went on every night in the house at the bottom of the street.

"I'm gonna have some weird dreams tonight," Tim said quietly.

"Nightmares," Ella added.

"Yeah, nightmares," Tim said.

"Aw, no!" Jack said. Someone was making their way towards them. Even through the thick darkness, Jack knew only one person who walked quite like that: determined, quick and springy, like the antelopes in wildlife documentaries. "That's Mum."

As she approached, Jack's mother searched their faces, as if looking for something in them. She took Jack's face in her hands, a hand on each cheek, as if soaking up the very sight of him. "You're okay," she said. "All of you. And Edmund. Good."

No one spoke.

"Did you see it?" Jack's mum asked.

Tim, Jack and Ella nodded.

"And?"

"It's a massive thing, like an ape, but bigger," Jack said.

"The Maero," Jack's mother said. "So it still comes. How can that man live with his conscience?"

"Mr Thompson?" Tim asked.

"Yes. Never mind. Let's go home."

"Mum, Edmund—"

"It's late. You all need to get to bed. Ella and Tim, your parents are very worried. Tomorrow we'll talk about how you went without our permission, and tomorrow we'll talk about the Maero."

Jack hadn't slept well. Even the ruru softly cooing in the tree through the night hadn't helped. He'd dreamt that Edmund had been torn limb from limb by the Maero and that he'd been eaten: fur, bones, everything. All Jack had been able to take home with him was Edmund's tail. At 6:15 a.m., Jack gave up on sleep. He sat up in bed to think about the facts. It was clear the Maero came to Mr Thompson's every night. He yelled, shouted and cried. The question was, why?

Jack's stomach rumbled and he quietly made his way out of his bedroom to go and get some breakfast. Edmund was lying in the hallway. As Jack bent down to stroke him, the dog's tail thumped loudly on the wooden floor. "Hey boy, I was wrong about you, wasn't I? You're a super-hero. You went out to face that baddie all by yourself."

Jack straightened and continued into the kitchen. As he poured cornflakes into a bowl, Edmund padded in and sat heavily in the doorway, watching him. "The thing is, Edmund," Jack continued, "that Maero isn't like other baddies. In the movies, baddies are just baddies, like the Joker in Batman. But that Maero didn't hurt you. He could have killed you, but he didn't."

The only sound that came from Edmund was his tail beating joyfully on the floor.

"You're a good listener, Edmund," Jack said between mouthfuls of cornflakes. "Maybe that's why the Maero liked you." Jack took another spoonful of cornflakes and chewed and crunched, then stopped. He lowered his spoon and stood up. "That's *it*, Edmund. You *listened* to the Maero. That's why he didn't hurt you. He's trying to tell us something and you sat and listened to him till he was finished."

Soundlessly, Jack ran back to his bedroom. He changed into his T-shirt and shorts then quietly let himself out the front door. It was time to wake up Ella and Tim. With Edmund breathing heavily beside him, he made his way to the house next door then the house across the road.

First, they searched for the word 'Maero' on the internet at Tim's house. The full name appeared to be Maeroero. According to Maori folklore, it came out at night and lived in the forest.

"Like the patupaiarehe," Tim said.

"Thought you didn't believe in fairies," Ella said.

"I thought I didn't either," Tim answered, "but the last couple of days have been …" Tim wasn't sure of the right word to use.

"Unusual," Ella said, finishing his sentence for him.

"Look," Jack said. "The Maero can tear a person apart with its sharp claws."

"No wonder your mum didn't want us to go there," Tim said.

"But he didn't touch Edmund," Ella said.

"And," Tim added, "it says here that they are afraid of water, not like the patupaiarehe. If he's afraid of water, how come he steps over the creek?"

"The creek's hardly got any water in it, so it's probably not that frightening," Jack suggested.

"I think," Ella said, "that whatever the Maero was trying to tell Edmund was more important than his fear of water."

"But Mr Thompson refuses to listen to him," Tim added.

"Time to ask Mum some more questions," Jack said. "Let's go to my house."

"I haven't had breakfast yet!" Tim protested.

"Have some at my house."

"Is your mum still angry about last night?"

"Yep, but she said she wants to think about what happened, talk about it with Dad and then talk with me," Jack said. "I hate it when she keeps me hanging like that."

"Dad said I have to wash the car and mow the lawns for lying," Tim said.

"And I'm not allowed to play outside after dinner for a week," Ella added.

"Hmmm," Jack said. "And I have to wait. Hate that."

Leaning over his bowl of cornflakes, Tim listened to Jack's mother. She explained how the Maero had torn down Mr Thompson's grandfather's dam, but the water hadn't returned.

"So why didn't the water come back?" Tim asked.

Very slowly, Jack's mum answered, "The old people – my grandparents, too – said the Maero put a curse on it."

"A curse?" Ella's eyes widened. "But curses can be lifted, can't they?"

Aroha, Jack's little sister interrupted. "Mum, Edmund's scratching at the door."

"Well, let him out, Aroha. He probably wants to go to the toilet."

"But the Maero got what he wanted by smashing down the dam," Ella continued. "Yet still he didn't lift the curse. There must be something else he wanted too." Ella twisted her hair around her pen and gazed out the window towards the trees Jack's mum had planted around the creek. Edmund was running, surprisingly quickly, around the trees. They were quite tall now. Some had leaves stained orange-red by autumn, like lipstick smudges. Some were native trees with tui searching their flowers for nectar. The fruit trees were her favourite, especially the feijoas, but there were guava, peach, apple and apricot trees. Ella smiled as she watched Edmund standing up on his hind legs scratching at the trees. He obviously loved them as much as Jack's mum did, as much as the tiny forest fairies did, as much as …

Ella let go of her hair. The pen unravelled and clattered on to the table. "He wants the trees back!" she blurted. "It's where they all lived, isn't it? He wants the forest back."

"The forest!" Tim choked slightly on his cornflakes. "Like the patupaiarehe."

"Mr Thompson hasn't got *any* trees," Jack added. He looked at his father. "It's like the orangutans and the palm trees, Dad. Remember that documentary?"

Jack's father nodded. "I do, Jack."

"Looks like Edmund's giving you a clue," Jack's mother said. "What are you going to do about it?"

"But you said you didn't want us to have anything more to do with the Maero!" Jack said.

"Yes, that's true. But if planting trees will lift the curse and bring our creek back to life – *and* get rid of the Maero once and for all, I may need to change my mind." Jack's mum raised her eyebrows expectantly. "You'd better get on with it or you'll never get this nature rescue project finished. Rinse your plates first …"

The three friends worked out a plan. The first step was to advertise the tree-planting weekend and fundraise. Next, they needed to get the support of all the Tui Street residents. Finally, they would have to clean all the rubbish out of the river and plant the trees. Of course, they couldn't mention things like the Maero or the patupaiarehe because people might think they were making it all up or trying to scare them into saving the creek.

The flyers had a photo of the creek showing a supermarket trolley, tyre and litter in it. The heading read: 'WAIMOE – OUR SLEEPING BEAUTY'. Beneath that was: *Would you like our Tui Street creek to be healthy again? This is your chance to help. We need trees, especially native trees. Lots of trees will bring back bird life. We also need your help to clear out the rubbish. Who knows? Maybe one day water will run through our creek again. Can you help us give the kiss of life to our hidden Beauty?*

They put Jack's phone number on the flyers. For the next week, every day after school they walked around local businesses and houses and delivered them into letterboxes or directly into people's hands.

Tim's father suggested they phone the local newspaper, which resulted in an article about the Tui Street Creek Rescue Project. Ella's stepmother, Serena, suggested they phone the local radio station, and all three children were invited to speak about their project on the breakfast show. Mr Tāmati, who had set the nature rescue project assignment, asked them to speak at assembly and suggested that all students could bring in a gold coin donation to help buy trees.

The hardest thing was trying not to mention the Maero. He had become as important to the project as the creek itself. Each needed the other. The Maero needed Waimoe to have her forest back, and the creek needed the Maero to lift the curse.

The second step was fairly simple: to get people on the creek side of Tui Street to agree to have trees planted at the bottom of their gardens along the edges of the creek. Luckily, most people had already heard about the rescue project and everyone was keen.

Everyone except Mr Thompson.

"If trees are there," he told the children, "I won't be able to see that ape-creature coming. I don't want him lurking in the shadows."

"We think the Maero will stop coming once he knows we've respected his wishes," Ella explained. "He'll probably never come back again if you let us plant lots of trees at the bottom of your back yard."

"How would you know what his wishes are?"

Tim stepped in to help. "The thing is, we can't promise that we're right, but we think trees are what the Maero wants. If we replant, we think he'll let the water run again and he'll leave you alone forever."

"Hmmm." Mr Thompson scratched his head. "Y'know what? I don't want to plant trees. I haven't been down that part of my back yard in years. Too scared I'll get mauled to death by that mad ape-thing."

"We can do the planting for you then," Jack said. "Just think, Mr Thompson, if we're right and the Maero does go away, you can use your back yard again."

"You could sit out there in the shade of the trees in the summer," Ella added. "You could even have a hammock there, like my friend Lucy."

Mr Thompson opened his mouth, so that his few teeth, gums and tongue were all they could see. Out of his mouth came a gurgling sound, as if someone were trying to start a car in his throat. For a moment Ella was afraid that her hammock idea had made him choke with anger, until Jack nudged her in the ribs. "He's laughing," he whispered.

Mr Thompson closed his mouth. "Ah, that was good. Haven't laughed like that for a long time. Now, can't stand round here all day talking to you lot. Got things to do. Anyway, haven't you got a hammock you should be swinging on?" His mouth opened and the car-trying-to-start sound began in his throat again.

"Mr Thompson," Ella said firmly. "There's something you should know." She waited until he'd stopped laughing.

"Is there now?" he said, the snarl returning.

"That ape-thing has a name. He's called a Maero. He's been mourning for his habitat, which your grandfather destroyed."

Mr Thompson scratched his head again. "Is that right? Well, shame I'm gonna leave it destroyed then, isn't it?" He turned to go in his front door then turned back. "You come near this house with trees and I'll set the dogs on you. Now get off my property."

Planting weekend was getting closer. Trees appeared from everywhere. Mr Tāmati had collected enough money at school to buy forty trees, and businesses and people in the neighbourhood had donated even more. The mayor herself donated ten native trees.

On the Saturday of planting weekend, a pleasing number of volunteers turned out to clean up the creek. Some rubbish was recyclable, like cans and bottles; some went straight to the dump, like an old gumboot, a broken television and a three-legged chair. Two rusty supermarket trolleys were pulled out and wheeled back to Awatiu shopping centre.

Jack's mother decided to clean the area of creek at the bottom of Mr Thompson's back yard. Ella, Tim and Jack helped her fill a wheelbarrow with creek rubbish, while Edmund lay nearby in a sunny spot.

"So, this is where the Maero comes every night?" Jack's mum said.

"Yep, he steps over the creek here," said Tim, "even though he's scared of water."

"Not much water to be scared of though, Tim. Just a dirty puddle really."

"Might not be like that for long if the Maero lifts his curse," Ella said, tossing something that looked like an old slipper into the wheelbarrow.

"Oi! Get off my property!" a voice boomed. Mr Thompson stood at his back door. "You are trespassing!"

Jack's mother looked up at Mr Thompson. "Morning, Mr Thompson!" she called. Under her breath, she said, "Keep going, children."

"Ignoring me, eh? Wonder if you'll ignore the police. Is that what you want – the police?"

"Mr Thompson, we are not on your property," Jack's mum called. "We are simply cleaning out the creek."

Mr Thompson stared at her. "I'll set the dogs on you!"

"I think you'll find we have a fairly brave guard dog right here, Mr Thompson." Jack's mum pointed at Edmund. "Now, we have lots to do. Please let us get on with it – unless you'd like to join us?"

"Think you're doing such a good deed, don't you? You come onto my property to plant trees tomorrow and I'll call the police. Hear me?"

Jack's mother looked up at him. "I think the whole neighbourhood can hear you, Mr Thompson."

The next day was Sunday, planting day. People turned up with spades and gumboots. Some of them were people who had read about the project in the newspaper or a flyer in their letterbox, people who just wanted to help. From nine in the morning they worked, stopping only for lunch. The Tui Street residents brought tea, coffee, sandwiches, cakes and biscuits out onto the street for the workers to eat. People took time out and sat on deck chairs and picnic rugs, chatting and laughing.

After lunch, Jack's mother stepped forward and asked for silence. "We're nearly there, I think," she said. "In fact, every back yard on the creek side now has a thick forest of trees at the creek's edge. There's still one back yard we haven't done though, at the very end of Tui Street – Mr Thompson's house."

"Let's do it!" a man called. "It'll only take ten minutes with all of us."

Jack's mum nodded. "You're right. The difficulty is that Mr Thompson refuses to let us plant at the bottom of his section."

People began to talk. The volume of the chatter rose. Jack's mother put her hand up in the hope that people might quieten. "Anyone got any ideas?"

Ella's dad spoke. "What do the kids think? It's their project. Ella, any thoughts?"

Ella climbed down from her perch beside Lucy on the wall outside Terri's house. "We want to plant trees along the whole of the Tui Street Creek. We want to make her as healthy as possible."

"Let's do it then," Ella's dad said. "I'm sure we can convince Mr Thompson."

Jack's mother shook her head at Ella's dad. "The thing is, Mr Thompson is not very friendly."

"He's got crazy dogs," Jack said.

Tim's dad stood up and picked up his spade. He walked over to the pile of potted trees on the footpath and picked one up. "I'm heading up there to plant some trees. Anyone joining me?"

The crowd of people stood, picking up spades and trees, and began to walk up Tui Street. No one stopped at Mr Thompson's gate. No one took much notice of the 'Beware of the Dogs or 'No Trespassing' signs. They walked straight through the gate and down the driveway.

Mr Thompson came out of his front door. "Get off my land!" he shouted.

In his hand he carried a slug gun.

"We're here to do a community service," Ella's dad said. "We'd like you to join us."

Mr Thompson lifted the gun.

Jack's mum stepped forward. "We're only planting trees, Mr Thompson."

"I'll call the police!" Mr Thompson called.

Jack's father stepped up beside his wife. "I think

the police might be more interested in the way you're threatening your neighbours with a gun, Mr Thompson."

Snarling, Mr Thompson pointed the gun at Edmund. "Leave now, or the dog gets it."

Jack looked down at Edmund, sitting quietly by his side. His head was at an angle, watching Mr Thompson, as if trying to understand his actions.

Everyone held their breath. Surely he wouldn't shoot a dog? Mr Thompson's finger moved, slowly and carefully, to pull the trigger. As he pressed, people screamed. A shot resounded through the crisp, autumn air.

"No! No!" Jack yelled, sprinting towards Mr Thompson. Beside him, Edmund ran and leapt at the man, knocking him backwards. The gun flew out of his hand.

Mr Thompson stood, empty-handed, glaring at the dog. Jack stood frozen on the step below him and Edmund sat on the gun. People quietened. Panic stopped. No one was hurt.

Mr Thompson laughed unkindly. "The gun's not loaded anyway."

Jack's mother spoke quietly. "We are going to plant trees now, Mr Thompson," she said.

Without speaking, the crowd of people filed past

Mr Thompson, through the gate, and down towards the creek. His dogs barked and strained at their leashes at the invasion.

Jack's parents and Ella and Tim went straight to Jack, who hadn't moved. His heart banged in his chest. He looked at Mr Thompson. "That's our dog," he said, bending down to pull Edmund to him.

Behind Jack, his father reached down and pulled the gun out from under Edmund. "People like you shouldn't have guns."

"Give me that!" Mr Thompson said, stepping towards Jack's dad.

"If you don't let him take that gun," Ella said, "I'm going to tell everyone that you're scared of an imaginary Maero."

"That ape-thing isn't imaginary."

"Yeah, we know that," Ella said, "but the others don't."

Mr Thompson's lip curled back. He bared his teeth, like one of his dogs, but he said nothing.

Tim put his hand under Jack's elbow. "See ya, Mr Thompson," he said, as he led Jack down the steps to join the others.

Behind them, Jack could hear his dad saying that he'd take the gun to the police station later and let them decide what to do with it.

Gradually, trees took root in the bare back yard. Bit by bit, a forest began to grow.

The Save our Tui Street Creek nature rescue project scored high marks from Mr Tāmati.

The Maero still came to Mr Thompson's but no longer made any sound. He would sit among the small trees for a while, then stand slowly and disappear into the distance. After that, he seemed to be coming just to check on the trees each night. Soundlessly, he walked over the creek, looked at the trees, turned around and walked away.

One night, some months later, he stopped coming altogether. Mr Thompson hovered at the window, TV turned up loud, lights off as always, so he could see out into the night. He waited and wondered and waited and wondered. After all these years, the Maero had gone.

That same night, another sound came through Jack's bedroom window. It wasn't the ruru. It wasn't the soft chatter of his parents in their bedroom, or Aroha talking in her sleep across the hallway. It was a sound Jack didn't recognise. He climbed out of bed and went into his parents' bedroom.

"There's a funny sound," he said.

"What do you mean?" Jack's mum asked.

"Oh, I don't know. It's just ..." Jack turned and walked down the hallway, followed by his parents and Edmund. He walked through the kitchen and opened the back door.

At the bottom of the garden, patupaiarehe sparkled in the branches of the trees, swooping down into the creek and coming up with water glistening on their wings and dripping from their tiny bodies.

"Water!" Jack's voice was loud and his mum didn't tell him to lower it.

Instead, she joined in: "Waimoe! She's awake!"

They ran down to the creek. Below them, water sighed joyously. The ripples winked merrily as they whooshed past over the litter-free creek bed. The air smelt fresh and clean.

"I have to tell Ella and Tim!" Jack said. Before his mum could tell him it was too late to go anywhere, he'd gone. She needn't have worried though. It seemed the whole street was stirring. Neighbours in their dressing gowns and pyjamas were coming out of their houses. The thrill in their voices created a happy hum alongside the rush of water in the Tui Street creek. People laughed and hugged.

"Look," Jack said.

At the bottom of the street, Mr Thompson stood

on his front steps. He stayed for some time, watching everyone. Noticing Jack, Tim and Ella, he nodded at them before turning and walking back inside.

Tim, Ella and Jack were the last to leave Waimoe's side that night. It was hard to pull their gaze away from the water as it journeyed past them, reflecting soft moonlight and patupaiarehe.

"Wonder where he's gone?" Jack said, looking across the creek into the distance.

"The Maero?" Tim asked. "I was thinking about him too." He looked across the creek into the darkness beyond.

"At least he can relax now," Ella said. "He doesn't need to worry about Tui Street anymore."

Jack grinned. "And Mr Thompson won't have that 'ape-thing' visiting either."

Ella raised her eyebrows. "Now he can go lie on his hammock!"

They laughed and, leaving the water flowing behind them, turned and made their way slowly back to their homes, to bed.

Cloudbird

IN A TWO-STOREY HOUSE near the entrance to Tui Street lived Louie, a boy who never played outside. His house was painted a crisp white and green, with orderly pot plants carefully placed on the front porch. The front yard was neat and tidy. Gardens were weeded. The bird bath was full of water. Even the puriri tree, tall and wide, with its determined red flowers, was pruned regularly to keep it in hand. Everything was neatly arranged, like a line drawn so straight, it could have been done with a ruler.

Louie often looked out from his window on the top floor and waved at Jack, Tim and the other Tui Street kids as they passed on their skateboards and bikes. They could see him, alone at his desk, gazing out at the goings-on in the street. From the footpath they couldn't see the tui that often perched on Louie's windowsill, keeping him company. Louie called the tui Cloudbird, because it looked as if a small piece of cloud had attached itself to his neck while he'd been flying one day and had remained there forever.

Louie lived with his Mum, who didn't encourage him to go outside and join in with the other kids. She preferred him to stay at home. He played with the other kids when he was at school, but his mother drove him to and from school every day. Each morning she dropped him off at the school gate. At the end of each day, Louie walked slowly to meet her. His shoulders, which had nudged soccer players aside during lunchtime games, would begin to sink. Soon he would drive past his Tui Street friends laughing and chatting as they walked home from school.

One day, Mr Tāmati told the class they were going on a short walk. "A very short walk," he said, "so don't get too excited."

In lines, the class made their way to the school gate with Mr Tāmati leading the way. "Here we are," he said, waiting for everyone to quieten down before he continued. Then, with a serious expression on his face, he began, "This area is very busy in the morning, isn't it?"

The students nodded.

"I actually think it's become dangerous." Mr Tāmati paused. "Why do you think it might be dangerous?"

"Too many cars?" Lucy ventured.

Mr Tāmati nodded. "There are far too many cars." His eyes scanned the students, who'd arranged themselves in a semi-circle around him. "How many of you walk to school?"

Lucy, Tim, Ella, Terri, Jack, Gemma and Harry put their hands up. They lived in Tui Street, which wasn't too far from school. Children from other nearby streets also put their hands up.

"One day," Mr Tāmati continued, "there could be an accident. Too many cars and not enough parking spaces mean that parents do risky things. They pull into driveways to drop kids off and then back out, without always seeing children walking behind them."

Jack put his hand up. "Some kids are killed in their own driveways like that."

"Yes, it's a tragedy." Mr Tāmati looked around the entrance to the school gate. "Fact is, there's not enough room for all the cars to park, so what do we do about it? How do we prevent an accident?"

"Walk to school," Tim suggested, "if we live close enough."

Ella added, "That's better for the environment anyway. Sometimes, the exhaust fumes are so strong around here, I try not to breathe in."

Mr Tāmati nodded. "How many of you live close to school?" he asked.

Many hands shot up.

"Well, my challenge to you is that you walk to school for a whole month," Mr Tāmati said. "Those of you who don't live nearby, see if you can find another way to use the car less. Talk about it with your parents tonight and let the class know how you plan to do this tomorrow. If we can get all of you walking instead of using the car every day for a month, I'm going to organise a day trip to the hot pools. They've got new waterslides, I've heard, and their hotdogs are the best I've ever tasted. I'm going to put a chart on the wall, with your names on it. Put a tick beside your name each morning and afternoon that you walk. The challenge begins in one week, next Wednesday, the first day of the month. Remember – it has to be every day for a month for us to go to the hot pools."

As the Tui Street friends walked home from school that day, they discussed Mr Tāmati's challenge.

"We all have to walk to school though," Tim said, "and Louie isn't allowed to walk, so it'll never work."

"Maybe we should talk to his mum," suggested Ella. "We could explain the challenge."

"It's really not fair, anyway," Gemma said. "Why would she stop him doing stuff all the time?"

"Maybe she has some kind of power over him," Lucy said, "like mind control!" Everyone laughed.

"He's like a prisoner," Harry said quietly. "Stuck in his room all the time."

Terri, dribbling her soccer ball as they walked, stopped still. "If that was me, I'd climb out the window."

"He hasn't got long hair to climb down on," Jack said.

Tim's eyelid twitched uncomfortably. "This isn't Rapunzel, Jack."

"Come on, Timbo. Look at the facts. He's stuck up in his room and not allowed out." Unable to resist the ball at Terri's feet, Jack ducked in from Terri's left side and stole the ball from her. "Yes!" he exclaimed, quickly dribbling the ball away.

"Not for long!" Terri yelled, sprinting after him. Tiny as she was, she swept the ball from him with just a flick of her foot.

Ella smiled, watching Jack struggle to get the ball back from Terri. "Terri would definitely climb out the window," she said. "She'd go crazy not being able to play soccer."

Tim nodded. He would go crazy if he couldn't play soccer too.

"Hey," Lucy said, "what about if we climbed up to him instead?"

Jack, who'd given up trying to tackle the ball from Terri, ran back to join them. "We could get caught," he said. "Louie's mother's pretty strict. She doesn't even let him eat biscuits."

"No biscuits – ever?" Harry stopped walking. They were at the corner of Tui Street now.

Tim looked at Jack. "Imagine if your mother never made chocolate brownie." Jack frowned.

Tim kicked a stone that made a frustrated clink against a rock wall before it fell to the grass verge. "Let's give Louie some biscuits," he said. "We'll throw them up to him through his window. Tonight!"

The seven friends looked at each other.

"Better not get caught," Jack said.

"I'll get the biscuits," Ella said. "Serena won't mind if I take some from our pantry."

"Okay," Jack agreed, nodding. "Meet outside Ella's house at seven. Don't be late."

Suddenly, Terri stuck her small leg out in front of Jack, tripping him slightly. "Stop telling us what to do, Jack!"

That night, the wind rose and blew noisily around the lamp posts and the houses. Gates creaked and trees groaned. It felt like winter had decided to sneak back and pay a visit on spring. The friends met outside Ella's house, bundled up in warm jackets. Edmund sat among them, listening patiently to the whispers of the small group huddled around him.

"Need a stone to throw at the window," Jack said, picking up a stone the size of the palm of his hand.

Tim eyed the stone uncertainly. "Not that big, Jack. Might smash his window."

"True," Jack said, throwing the stone down. "Need a smaller one."

"C'mon, let's go," Terri said. "We'll find a stone on the way."

Two houses down was Louie's house. The light was on in Louie's room, but the window was shut. The curtains were open though and the seven Tui Street kids below could see Louie sitting at his desk. They hid behind the trunk of the large puriri tree in Louie's garden. Under the tree, oblivious to the wind, lay Edmund.

"Probably doing homework," Ella said, looking up at Louie. "All that stuff Mr Tāmati gave us – making graphs to show how many cars, bikes and stuff go past in one hour."

"We're gonna do that in the weekend," Gemma said, "outside the mall. Lots of traffic round there."

Edmund suddenly leapt to his feet and began to bark. Above, in the huge puriri tree, was Louie's tui friend, busily siphoning nectar from the puriri flowers.

"No, Edmund, no!" Jack whispered loudly. "Louie's mum will hear you. Edmund, sit! Sit!"

Edmund sat as directed, but his eyes stayed fixed on the bird.

"He doesn't normally bark at birds," Jack said. He looked up at the tui. It had stopped drinking. With a quick glance at Jack, it flew off towards Louie's window.

They waited for a few minutes, eyes fixed

anxiously on the front door. Luckily, Louie's mother didn't come out to see what the barking was about.

"Guys, we need to hurry up," Terri whispered. "It's getting dark and I've got to finish the dishes. I promised I'd be back in half an hour. Let's throw the biscuits to him now."

The window seemed a long way up. The stone in Jack's hand was light and he aimed it at the window sill. It hit the wood below the window with a small 'thunk'.

Louie looked up. He stood, leaning over his desk, to look through the window.

"He can probably only see his reflection cos his light's on," Harry said. "Throw another stone."

Lucy bent down. "Here's one. I'll throw it."

This time, Louie stood up and walked around his desk to open the window. He looked out into the blue-grey of the evening, his red hair lit up by the desk lamp beside him. "Who's there?"

"It's us!" Tim called quietly.

"We brought some biscuits," Ella said. She held the packet of biscuits up high, so that he could see them.

"Biscuits? Why?"

"Thought you'd like some," Jack whispered loudly, grinning.

"They might break if you throw them up this far," Louie said, grinning back.

The friends looked at each other. Terri, thinking quickly because she had to get home, noticed that one of the puriri tree branches wasn't too far from Louie's window. If someone climbed the tree and shimmied along the branch, they'd be able to throw the biscuits up to him without breaking any, hopefully.

"I've got an idea," Terri said and she began to explain, pointing to the branch.

"I had exactly the same idea!" Jack said. Terri looked at him. Jack laughed. "I did! I probably had the idea before you did!"

"Did not!"

"Did!"

Terri rolled her eyes, smiling. If she had her soccer ball right now, she'd let him think he could tackle it from her, then, just as he thought he had it, she'd flick it away from him and take off. Eventually, he'd say, "You're so good!" in his annoyed but admiring way.

Ella whispered, "I'm happy to climb up."

"I'll go with you," Tim said quietly. "It's getting dark and Dad says two sets of eyes are better than one."

Ella moved quickly and quietly; Tim scrambled behind. It wasn't long before Ella was at the end of the branch. Lucy, waiting beneath the branch, tossed the biscuits up to her.

Ella caught them gently then pushed herself up onto all fours. "Stay there, Tim, in case I wobble." Slowly and slightly shakily, she stood up on the branch, holding the biscuits up in the dim light so that Louie could see.

"Watch out for my little mate," Louie called gently.

"What did you say?" Ella cocked her ear towards Louie.

"Cloudbird, watch out for him." Louie pointed at the tui sitting on the windowsill as he leant out.

"A tui!" Ella put her hand over her mouth, realising she'd spoken a little too loudly. Louie nodded. Ella smiled. "He's so tame. Okay, I'll aim to your left." Gently she threw the packet of biscuits to Louie.

Catching the biscuits with both hands, Louie smiled back at her. "Thanks, Ella. Thanks, Tim." Looking down at the others, he whispered loudly, "Got them!" and held the biscuits up for them to see. "Better go. Mum's coming up the stairs. She hates biscuits." Louie dipped back inside and closed the window. With a small wave of his hand, he moved away out of sight, leaving his curtains wide open. From below, his window looked like a large open eye, surrounded by other windows with their eyelids closed.

Louie's mum had never planned to be so strict, however, for many years, she and her husband hadn't been able to have children. As they had grown older, they had consoled themselves that at least they had each other. It had been a joyous occasion when they discovered they were going to become parents.

On the day that Louie was born, his parents realised no one else could ever matter to them as much as he did. Louie's dad, a quiet man who never expressed his feelings openly, laughed and cried with happiness when Louie was born. He became someone who smiled a lot and chatted with neighbours. He proudly pushed Louie in his pram, stopping to show him snails and butterflies as they walked.

One day, on his way to work, Louie's father stepped out in front of a car. It was rainy and difficult to see. The car's indicator showed it was supposedly turning right, but the driver changed his mind. The car was going too fast and there was no time for Louie's dad to step back to safety.

Louie had been too small to remember the phone ringing and how his mum's voice had quavered when she heard the news. He'd cried at the sound of the mug in her hand crashing to the floor. He'd been too little to remember his dad.

After Louie's dad had died, his mum vowed to protect Louie from every possible danger. She would keep him safe. She did not want to lose him like she'd lost his father.

At school the next day, Mr Tāmati asked again for the students who lived close to school to raise their hands. "Keep your hands up if you walked to school today," he said, scanning the raised hands. "We start the challenge in six days. If you didn't keep your hand up then you need to start thinking about walking to school very soon. Perhaps have a chat with your parents about this."

Louie looked out the window. He hadn't raised his hand. A large seagull flew onto the playground to pick up half a sandwich. He watched it soar up again with the crust dangling from its beak. He didn't think Mum would be willing to chat about walking to school. She thought the roads were too dangerous. It had been hard enough being driven when he was younger, at his old school. He hated the thought that he was going to let everyone in the class down with the walk-to-school challenge.

"You okay, Louie?" Tim asked, from his desk nearby.

"Yep." Louie nodded, but his eyes were heavy and worry seemed to be tugging at him, like an anchor keeping a boat from pulling free.

"Shall we bring more biscuits tonight?"

Louie smiled. He had eaten some of the biscuits and carefully saved some for another time. He opened his mouth to thank Tim again, but the words that had been making his head hurt tumbled out. "I'll never be allowed to walk to school, Tim. Mum won't let me."

That afternoon, Louie's mother was waiting in the car outside the school gate. She had the radio on and was listening to a man talking about some native dolphins that were endangered. When Louie got in the car, she turned the radio off.

"Hello, darling. How was your day?" she asked.

"Good." Louie clicked on his seatbelt, unwound the window and gazed out at the kids walking with their school bags slung over their shoulders.

"I've just been listening to the plight of that lovely dolphin, the endangered one. It's a native."

"The Maui dolphin."

"That's right, yes. The Maui dolphin. Quite small, aren't they?"

Louie didn't answer. He didn't feel like talking to his mother. All day at school he'd felt angrier and angrier. Every time he tried to push the anger away, it rolled back like a wave, frothy and restless and bubbling within him.

"Are they small?" his mum asked again. "I can't quite remember. Sometimes I get dolphin breeds muddled."

"Small," Louie said.

"Right. Yes." Louie's mother looked at him briefly, while trying to keep her eyes on the road. "Are you okay, Louie?"

"Yes."

"Are you sure? You seem—"

"I have to walk to school, Mum," Louie interrupted. "I have to walk to school and home from school."

Louie's mother was silent. Her hand reached for the indicator and pushed it firmly down. A little right arrow pulsed on the dashboard and the *click, click, click* sound filled the car.

Louie continued, "If we walk to and from school every day for a whole month, Mr Tāmati will take us on a trip to the hot pools. He thinks more kids should be walking cos he thinks it's dangerous having all the cars at the school gate." Louie turned towards his mother. "You're one of those parents, blocking everyone with this car."

Louie's mum stayed silent. She pressed the horn at someone in front who hadn't noticed the lights had turned green.

"I don't want you to drive me anymore," Louie said firmly. He turned back to the window and stared hard at the trees and the lampposts as they whizzed past. His hand shook slightly as it rested on the window frame. He could hear his pulse, as if he'd been running.

His mother pulled into their driveway and stopped the car. She took the keys out of the ignition and turned to Louie. "You're not walking to school," she said. "And that is final."

Louie went straight to his room and shut the door. He opened the window and sat gazing out at the street. He was always home before the other kids. Soon, Jack, Tim, Ella, Lucy, Terri and the twins would walk past his house. They'd wave up at him and he'd wave back, like they did every day. Today though, wasn't like every other day.

Looking down from his window, the puriri's

branch seemed too far down for him to reach. Ella had managed to stand on it, but she'd still had to throw the biscuits a fair distance up to him from there. He swung his legs over the windowsill, letting them dangle below him. Halfway out the window. Halfway to a decision. It was still too much of a drop from the window to the branch. He'd have to find something to hang on to. Hearing the voices of his school friends as they turned into Tui Street, he quickly swung his legs back inside the window. He would do it. He would definitely do it, but he needed more time to think it through.

From his branch nearby, Cloudbird flew to Louie's windowsill. His sleek, shiny feathers shimmered in the sun, as if green sea, black sand and blue sky had been sprinkled onto them. He sat beside Louie, facing into his bedroom.

"I need help," Louie told him. "I don't want to make Mum worry more, but I want to walk to school."

Cloudbird responded with two sounds at once: a clucking and a flute-like melody that spiralled gently around Louie's lonely heart. Louie turned to watch the tui as he sang. "How do you do that?" he asked.

The puff of white feathers, like cottonwool, trembled on the tui's neck as he sang.

"Is it the cloud on your neck?" Louie asked. "Is it filled with music?" Louie reached out. He'd never touched Cloudbird before, but the tuft of cloud on his neck seemed to invite a pat, like a cat that rubbed itself against your legs. With his index finger, Louie touched Cloudbird's neck. The tui was immediately still and soundless. Bit by bit, the tuft of white feathers under his neck began to puff up, larger and larger, until it was as big as Louie's hand. Cloud-soft feathers unfurled like one long, narrow quilt of candyfloss. Down from the windowsill it tumbled, until it reached the floor.

"Wh-what just happened?" Louie asked Cloudbird. Very slowly and carefully, he placed his hand around the waterfall of feathers. Each feather appeared to be bound to another, as if matted together with glue.

Louie tugged the stream of white feathers. It was definitely attached firmly to Cloudbird's neck. He didn't want to tug too hard, in case his small friend was pulled from the windowsill with the pressure. However, the opposite seemed to happen. When he tugged the feathers, Cloudbird grew to the size of a seagull. With another tug, he was the size of a duck. With the weight of each tug, the tui grew, his weight balancing constantly.

As Louie hung on to the flowing blanket of white with both hands, he realised that Cloudbird, now the size of an ostrich, would be able to hold him if he climbed out the window. A few moments later, Louie was dangling, feet against the outside of the house, abseiling down the wall, with Cloudbird holding him steady from above, as tall and wide as a moa. Looking up, it was hard to see Cloudbird properly. He was inside Louie's room and only the middle of his long, thickly-feathered body was visible from below.

Down Louie went, pushing away from the wall with his feet, swinging into the air, out over the garden to the street below. When his feet touched the ground, he stood for a moment and looked around him. Towering over him was the puriri tree. Beneath his feet was grass.

Gently, Louie released the white feather quilt. "Thanks, Cloudbird," he whispered up to the window above. He walked out of the gate and onto Tui Street. Instead of turning right and joining Jack, Tim and Terri practising soccer kicks on the long driveway at the bottom of the street, he turned left, making his way out of Tui Street, in the direction of school. Purposefully, he strode, stopping at the lights to cross at the pedestrian crossing, scanning driveways for reversing cars, humming to himself like a bird.

'Like a tui,' he thought to himself, smiling. In that moment, a small breeze swept past him and there was Cloudbird, his normal size again, flying from tree to tree beside him.

Mr Tāmati was still in their classroom, even though school had finished a couple of hours ago. He sat at his desk, his glasses perched on his nose, with a pile of exercise books beside him. Cloudbird perched on the jungle gym briefly before sweeping up into the kowhai tree, where he drank the nectar of the yellow, bell-shaped flowers. Mr Tāmati looked up suddenly, as if aware of the tui's movement. He stood and came to the classroom door, opening it and looking out. His gaze moved from Cloudbird to Louie, standing indecisively under the tree.

"You missing school so much you thought you'd come back for the night?" Mr Tāmati asked.

Louie smiled. "Just out for a walk," he answered.

"Your mum know you're out?" Mr Tāmati asked. Louie shook his head. "Hmmm." Mr Tāmati took his glasses off and rubbed his eyes.

"I'm okay though," Louie explained, pointing up to the tui above him. "I've got Cloudbird."

Mr Tāmati looked up at the tui. "Cloudbird," he said slowly. The tui stopped dipping his beak into kowhai flowers and turned to look at Mr Tāmati. He opened his mouth and with a soft click from behind his white tuft, he began to sing.

"Did you know tui have two voice boxes?" Mr Tāmati asked.

"No. I wondered how he did that, making two sounds at once."

"Birds can do all kinds of clever things."

"Like what?"

"Like building nests," Mr Tāmati said. "I especially like the way they share the care of their young. One bird flies off for food, while the other stays at the nest. Then they swap. They give each other breaks."

"What about growing bigger, changing shape? Ever seen a bird do that?"

Mr Tāmati looked at Louie for a moment. "I haven't, Louie. Have you ever seen that?"

Louie felt hot around his neck. This was like when Mr Tāmati asked him a question in class and he had to think quickly. "I ... er ... no. I just wondered if it was possible for a bird to sort of ... shape-shift."

"Old Maori stories tell of large birds. There was a bird, legend says a moa, who carried a homesick man called Pou-rangahou on his back, all the way from Hawaiki to Aotearoa, back to his wife and son. There was also a story of a bird woman called Kura, who took Hatupatu, a mischievous boy, in her claws like an eagle might, and flew with him. He managed to escape her though. She ended up dying in a boiling mud pool."

"Do you believe those stories, Mr Tāmati?"

"Do you, Louie?"

Louie bit his lip. "I think birds can change their size," he said.

"There is also a story of a pouakai, a large bird that would swoop down and carry people off to its nest, where it ate them. Some people say the warriors only managed to kill it because it was distracted by a man's red hair. When it attacked the man, it got its claws caught in his flax cape. As it tried to free itself, the group of warriors clubbed it to death."

Louie chewed his lip. "My hair is red, sort of," he said.

"Yes, well, we can all relax with you around then, Louie. You can distract any bird that plans to eat us, while we launch an attack," Mr Tāmati said. "An unlikely event though, I'd say."

Louie laughed, but a moment later his expression was serious again. "Maybe the large bird could help the redhead instead," he suggested.

Mr Tāmati nodded slowly. "Maybe. Maybe a large

bird *could* help the redhead." He took his glasses off, breathed steam on them and wiped them with his hankie. "You should go home now, Louie. Your mum will be worrying about you."

"Can't I stay here with you?" Louie asked. "I won't disturb you."

"I'll be going soon, Louie," Mr Tāmati said. "Like the birds, I'm the parent who gives his wife a chance to fly off for a while. My wife goes for a run when I get home, while I bath the tamariki. You head off now. I'll see you tomorrow."

Louie walked home slowly, as Cloudbird flew from tree to tree beside him. When they reached Tui Street, it was quiet. Louie guessed everyone had gone in for dinner. He wondered if his mum had been searching for him, calling for him to come and eat with her. When he reached his gate, it occurred to him that he couldn't just walk through the front door. His mother would wonder where he'd been. She'd be even angrier with him if she knew he'd sneaked out.

"Cloudbird?" he whispered loudly.

The tui glided from a branch in the puriri tree towards Louie, then hovered beside him. Louie reached out and gently tugged the white tuft under his neck. Again, the white quilt of feathers grew, and each time Louie pulled, Cloudbird grew larger and rose higher and higher, until he was level with Louie's open bedroom window. Climbing up the cloud of softness, Louie reached Cloudbird's neck, parallel to the window. Stretching out, he pulled himself up and slung his legs over. He was inside.

"Louie!" he heard his mother call. "Dinner's ready." He could hear her footsteps on the stairs.

Should he shut the curtains? It was still light, but she'd see a giant bird at his window! Turning frantically to look behind him, he stopped and let out a relieved breath. All she would see was a tui on the tree. Cloudbird had returned to his original size.

The door opened. "Oh, there you are," his mother said. "You didn't answer and I wondered if you'd snoozed off over your homework. Dinner's ready."

The next morning, Louie waited for his friends at the top of Tui Street. As they approached, talking and kicking Terri's soccer ball, they came to a surprised stop.

"You walking today?" Jack asked.

"Yep," Louie answered.

"To school?" Lucy asked.

"Yeah, but we'd better get going. Mum doesn't

know I've already left. She's still cleaning her teeth."

The eight Tui Street kids began to walk, Cloudbird fluttering in and out of branches beside them.

"Won't you get into trouble, Louie?" Tim asked.

"Don't care. I want to walk."

"Cool. We'll go to the hot pools now," Terri said. "But will you be able to walk every day? Will your mum let you?"

"I'm gonna walk every day," Louie replied. His red hair glistened under the sun. Up ahead, Cloudbird turned back and, seeing the red flame of hair, flew over Louie, low and close, as if to remind him he was there.

Harry began to flail his arms about in the air to frighten the bird away.

"No, don't do that. He's kind of a pet," Louie said. "He just sort of hangs out with me."

"You're so lucky," Ella said. "A pet tui!"

Louie wondered whether to tell them about how Cloudbird sort of shape-shifted, but decided not to. Perhaps walking to school with Cloudbird was enough for one day.

Back home, Louie's mother was concerned. Louie hadn't answered her when she'd called out that she was ready to go. Calling a number of times, she became worried. Quickly, she strode up the stairs and knocked loudly on Louie's door. In a panic, she flung the door open. Had Louie collapsed or had an electric shock? No. The room was empty. The bed was neatly made … and the window was wide open.

Louie's mum went into every room in the house searching for her son. By the time she was back downstairs, she knew he'd done exactly what she'd forbidden him to do. But how had he managed to get downstairs and leave the house without her hearing him?

Quickly, she grabbed her keys and ran to the car. What if he'd been bitten by a dog or fallen over and knocked his head … or what if …? She put her hand over her mouth as if it might stop her from thinking it. *What if he'd been hit by a car?* She couldn't bear to think of it, and shut her eyes for a moment to push out of her mind the image of Louie lying on the road, unconscious.

By the time she found a park, two streets away from the school, Louie's mother decided it would have been faster to walk. Often, when she dropped Louie off, she'd pull into a driveway just long enough for him to jump out, because there was nowhere to park. Now, she ran with her keys clinking in her coat pocket, her neatly arranged hair slipping from its clips. When she arrived at Louie's classroom, she felt less carefully put-together.

Mr Tāmati saw her first. He asked Jack to finish reading out the school notices for the day, while he stepped outside to talk with her.

"Louie is here, isn't he?" she asked, her breath tight in her chest.

"Yes, he's here. Right there." Mr Tāmati pointed through the window.

"Oh, thank goodness he's all right." Louie's mum let out a breath. "I'm sorry. I didn't mean to interrupt your teaching. I'll go."

Mr Tāmati reached out and put his hand on Louie's mother's arm. "Are you okay?"

"Yes, yes, fine. He just … ah … walked to school. I prefer to drive him."

From the kowhai tree, outside the classroom, a tui's song pierced the silence. Mr Tāmati looked over at the bird. He pushed his glasses up onto the ridge of his nose. "What does Louie prefer?" he asked.

Louie's mum dabbed her hair back, slipping strands back into clips. "It doesn't matter what Louie prefers, Mr Tāmati. I'm his mother and I think I know what's best for him. Now, I'd better let you get back to the class. Thank you. Have a good day."

Louie's mother turned and walked away. Mr Tāmati stood still for a moment. He could hear Jack reading out notices about choir practice in the hall at lunchtime. He looked at the tui. It was silent.

"Are you going to chase after her?" he asked. "She has red hair."

Cloudbird looked back at him, made a clucking sound and stuck his beak into a kowhai flower.

"Hmmm. I don't really blame you," Mr Tāmati said. "It's all rather tricky, isn't it?" He walked back into the classroom to the sounds of whispers, scraping chairs and Jack's voice, as he finished the notices. "Thanks Jack," he said.

Jack saluted Mr Tāmati. "At your service, sir!"

The class laughed.

"Hmmm. Might be time to get started on some maths," Mr Tāmati said, a small smile at the corners of his mouth.

Louie's mother woke up a bit earlier the next morning. When Louie heard her boiling the kettle, he quickly got dressed. When he heard the shower going, he ran downstairs, ate some cereal, took his lunchbox from the fridge and ran back upstairs to pack his bag. At the sound of his mum turning off the shower, he cleaned his teeth – a little less thoroughly than usual, because he didn't have much time. He knew his mother would be dressing and fiddling around with her hair and make-up and he needed that time to let Cloudbird in and then climb down the quilt of feathers.

Each morning that week, his mother waited downstairs for Louie, her keys at the ready, coat on and red hair neatly swept up with lots of small hairclips. Each morning, Louie had already climbed out of his window and walked to school with his friends. In the afternoon, he walked home with his friends. They'd pass his mum waiting in the car in a driveway, with the engine idling and exhaust fumes filling the air. She never called out to him. He knew she wouldn't embarrass herself in public. She just waited and eventually drove home again.

"How do you do it?" Terri asked one morning, dribbling her ball around trees and lamp posts, as they walked to school. "It's a big drop from your window to that branch."

"Yeah, how do you do that?" Ella asked.

"Maybe he flies!" Jack said, widening his eyes and lifting his eyebrows in mock horror.

"Maybe he teleports," Lucy suggested.

"One day, people *will* be able to teleport, y'know,"

Tim said. "I watched a documentary on it with Dad."

"Seriously, Tim? Teleport?" Gemma said. She raised a disbelieving eyebrow.

Ella intervened. "So, Louie, tell us – how do you get out of your window?"

"I've just worked out a way, that's all." Louie looked over at Cloudbird flying alongside them. He'd been walking to school for five days now. He knew it upset his mother, but he didn't feel he had a choice. If it hadn't been for Cloudbird, walking would never have been possible. Maybe, just maybe, they might get to go on the trip to the hot pools at the end of the month.

One morning, Louie's mum sat at the table, thinking. She knew now that Louie was not leaving the house through any downstairs exit. He did not go through the front door. He did not go through the back door. He was definitely leaving from upstairs. She suspected he was climbing through his window, but just couldn't think how he did it. There was only one way to find out.

She rinsed the breakfast dishes and left them on the bench. Upstairs, she turned on the shower and, though she hated to waste water, she left it running while she dressed. A few minutes later, she turned the shower off and slipped quietly out of the bathroom and down the stairs. Louie would think she was dressing now. Without making the slightest sound, she sneaked out the front door and hid behind the car in the driveway, watching Louie's window closely.

Upstairs, Louie hitched his schoolbag onto his back and opened the window. He could see Cloudbird on a branch outside. "Hey!" he called gently. The tui immediately flew to his windowsill.

Louie's mum watched as her son began to pull at the bird's cottony pouch of feathers. She gasped, hand over mouth, as the bird began to grow. She held her breath as Louie swung confidently down from his window, holding on to the long sheet of white feathers, like a rope. In a fit of panic, she stood, eyes wide with terror. Her fearful voice rang out through Tui Street. "Louie!" she screamed. "Hold on! Don't fall!"

Louie froze. Then, like dry sticky tape, Louie peeled backwards. His legs hit the branch as he fell and he landed heavily on his back. He made no sound. Louie's mother's screams ripped through the Tui Street morning.

The Tui Street kids had been heading up the street. When they heard the screams, they ran back down. Sprinting through Louie's gate and down to the puriri tree, they slowed, stopped and stared.

A super-sized bird was stretching its long neck downwards and nudging Louie with its beak. At a safe distance, Louie's mum was swatting at the bird with her handbag, screaming, "Get away from him! Get away from my son!"

"What is it?" Tim stopped and stared.

"It's ..." Ella began uncertainly, "it's a massive tui!"

The large bird gently nudged Louie onto its beak and tipped him down over its head and onto its back. Rolling over and over, Louie's eyes opened. He grabbed Cloudbird's neck to stop himself from falling.

"Louie!" his mother screamed.

The bird flapped its wings and rose into the air, its long, white-feathered tuft flowing from its neck like a beard. Louie felt the world tilt beneath him. He held on tightly to Cloudbird's neck, as his house and Tui Street became smaller. Below him, he could hear his mum screaming and the kids cheering and yelling.

"Don't worry, Mum!" he yelled. "He's my friend."

"Come back!" Louie's mother screamed. "Come down now!"

Louie was unable to respond. The cool air made his eyes sting and his mouth turn dry and wordless. There was his street, Tui Street, with the creek running to its left and the long driveway at the bottom with Terri's house beside it. There were Lucy, Tim, Jack and the twins' houses with Ella's and Louie's opposite.

"School!" Louie called to Cloudbird. "Let's go to school."

Up Tui Street they flew, over his friends pointing up at him, past the traffic lights where children with backpacks waited to cross, over the traffic piling up, like ants bungling and bumping around each other. There was the school gate, soccer field, teachers and students. There was the kowhai tree next to the jungle gym and Mr Tāmati walking across the playground to their classroom.

Louie yelled out, "Mr Tāmati, I'm riding a large bird, like the man in the story! Look, Mr Tāmati! I'm the redhead. The bird helped me!" His voice was swallowed by the wind. He watched as Mr Tāmati approached the classroom door then, just when Louie thought he was going to go inside, Mr Tāmati turned and looked up. He looked right at Louie and Cloudbird. Nudging his glasses further up his nose, he peered into the sky. He began to wave, his arm moving from side to side, big and wide. Louie imagined his smile broadening slowly. He couldn't see it, but somehow he knew it was there.

Cloudbird tipped upward and soared higher where the air was colder. Louie leant in to Cloudbird's feathers for warmth. Way below, Louie could see Tui Street again, as he and Cloudbird swerved from side to side, buffeted by thick pockets of air. Turning into the street, the large bird veered downwards and swung into Louie's front yard, landing on the lawn.

Louie's mother was standing exactly where she'd been when they left. She ran to them, her face pale, eyes swollen with crying. "Are you okay?" she asked. "Are you hurt?"

"I'm fine," Louie answered, gently easing himself off Cloudbird's back. Standing before his mum, he noticed the rings of worry under her eyes and saw her lip trembling as she bit back tears. She had seemed so tiny from up high and now, for the first time, he realised she was actually quite small and he was nearly as tall. She'd always been older than his friends' mums, but now she looked particularly old, and frightened.

"You don't need to worry, Mum," he said. "I'll be careful. I promise."

"You're not hurt?" his Mum asked. "That was so dangerous."

"It was fun, Mum," Louie said. He put his hand on her arm to reassure her. "I'll always look after myself y'know."

His mum patted his hand on her arm. "Louie, when I drive you to school, I know you've arrived there safely."

Louie felt that familiar, restless anger. He stepped back, almost tripping over Cloudbird, who was slowly returning to his original size.

"I just want to be normal," Louie said. "I want to walk to school with my friends. Think about how I feel, Mum." He walked over to Terri, Ella, Lucy, Gemma, Harry, Jack and Tim. "Come on," he said to them. "Let's go." Turning back to his mother, he added, "Please don't come to pick me up from school today, Mum, cos I'm walking home."

Louie's friends didn't move. Their eyes were fixed on Cloudbird.

"He's shrinking!" Jack said. "He's turning back into a normal tui."

"But how?" Terri asked. "How?"

Louie's friends looked at him.

"I dunno," Louie said, shrugging his shoulders. "He just grows. Don't tell anyone, guys. I wasn't even going to tell you until Mum ruined it all this morning." Louie turned back briefly and called,

"Come on, Cloudbird!"

The tui flew ahead of them and waited on top of a hedge by the gate. The eight children followed. Behind them, Louie's mother stood, tears in her eyes. 'Think about how I feel,' Louie had said to her. She nodded silently to herself. She would try, she thought. She would definitely try. Slowly, she turned and walked back into the house.

That afternoon, amidst the mad flurry of parents picking up their children from school, there was one less car. Louie's mother was not waiting in the car outside the school gate. Mr Tāmati was on gate duty, politely telling parents not to park on yellow lines and reminding children to watch out for cars swinging unexpectedly out of driveways. He nodded at Louie and his friends as they made their way out of the school gate. "Walking home again?"

"Yeah," Louie answered.

"I guess we'll be having a day at the pools, then," Mr Tāmati said.

On a branch behind Louie, Cloudbird launched into song.

"How's your little friend?" Mr Tāmati nodded towards Cloudbird.

"Good."

Cloudbird sang, clicking, clucking and piping two melodies at once.

"Sometimes I think I could listen to that all day," Mr Tāmati said.

"Shame humans haven't got two voice boxes, eh Mr Tāmati," Lucy said. "We could have two conversations at once."

"Hmmm, you lot are noisy enough with just one voicebox. Think I'd go mad if you had two."

"We'd go mad if you gave us two instructions at once too, Mr Tāmati," Jack said, grinning.

"Well, how about one instruction then: go home safely and I'll see you tomorrow."

The children laughed, said goodbye, and set off for Tui Street.

"Louie," Mr Tāmati called after him.

Louie turned round. "Yes?"

"You may find that now things have changed, other things might stop."

"Do you mean … ?" Louie looked at Mr Tāmati. "You mean no more … ?" He didn't know how to finish the question.

"I mean, Louie," Mr Tāmati explained, "that you're walking to school now. Things have worked out. Help comes when it's needed."

Louie nodded slowly. "Okay. See you tomorrow."

Mr Tāmati waved, moving quickly across the footpath to catch a pushchair rolling away from a distracted mother.

That night, Louie's mother told him that she would no longer insist on driving him to school. She asked only that he be extra careful crossing the roads.

Louie looked at his mum's tired, worried face. "I'll be very careful, I promise," he said.

The next morning, Louie called Cloudbird. As always, the tui flew to Louie's window and, as always, Louie chatted to his little friend. Swinging his schoolbag onto his back, he reached toward the white tuft on the little bird's neck. He stroked it gently for a moment. Holding it between his finger and thumb, he gave it a little tug. Nothing happened. He tugged it a little more. Nothing.

"Help comes when it's needed," Mr Tāmati had said. Louie ran his fingers over the tui's tuft one more time. "I guess I'll just go out the front door now then. See you downstairs, Cloudbird."

At the bottom of the stairs, Louie's mother passed him his drink bottle. "Have a good day," she said. "Don't forget your lunch."

"Got it," Louie said, kissing his mum's cheek.

"Louie—"

"Yes?"

His mother stood at the door. She didn't say anything.

"It's okay, Mum," Louie said. "I promised I'd be careful, remember?"

Closing the door behind him, Louie walked across the garden and through the gate to meet his friends on Tui Street. Beside him, Cloudbird dipped and swerved through branches. He sang two melodies, his joyous song bursting through the early Tui Street morning.

Lucy, the Pea and the Shaggy Dog Tree

IT WAS A TEACHER-ONLY DAY at Awatiu School, which meant the Tui Street kids had the day off. Tim's dad had to work, so Jack's mum was keeping an eye on him, while he and Jack built a tree hut in a large tangelo tree out the back of Tim's house. There was a stack of old decking wood in Jack's shed that his parents said they could use. The tangelo tree had two thick branches that were the same height, so the pieces of wood would easily lie flat between them. Sitting on a branch each, the two friends began to nail a platform on to the branches.

"At least we don't have to climb up high to build a platform, Jack," Tim said, looking up the driveway to the tall tree in Jack's front yard. "How'd your Mum do that?"

Jack shook his head. "She doesn't say much about it. Y'know what she's like."

"Yep," Tim said.

"She's made a big chocolate cake for later," Jack said. "I iced it, but Aroha had to help and she ate more icing than she put on."

Tim grinned. "I love your mum's chocolate cakes!"

"Hey, look!" Jack pointed over Tim's fence on the other side. Lucy was in her back garden. She had hedge-clippers and was hacking away at an overgrown bush, her brown pigtails jiggling with every snip. Further on, her father was weeding the vegetable garden and baby Tillie was sound asleep in a pushchair in the shade. Lucy's parents took turns at working and looking after the kids at home.

"Hey, Lucy," Tim called. "Helping your dad?"

Lucy squinted over at him, the sun her eyes. "Yeah, but it'll take ages. This bush is thick ... like Edmund's fur, Jack. Remember that time your grandma gave him a haircut?"

"Yeah, he looked awful after that. Felt sorry for him. I know he was hot with all that fur, but … hey! That bush you're cutting looks like a dog from here."

"Yeah," Tim agreed, "a dog that needs a haircut."

Lucy cocked her head and looked at the tree. It did look a bit like a dog. What if she made it the exact shape of a shaggy dog, with a tail, ears and a nose? "You're right, it does! I'm gonna cut it into a proper dog shape."

"Do you know," Lucy's dad joined in, "some people do cut trees into shapes? Chicken shapes, teddy bear shapes, the shape of aeroplanes … it's called 'topiary.' In England, there are old palaces and castles with trees cut into all kinds of shapes in the gardens. Kings, queens, princes and princesses must have really liked topiary."

"Hey, Dad – if I cut this tree into a shaggy dog shape, a princess might come to look at it," Lucy said. "It'll be that good!"

"Hmmm, it's unlikely, Luce." Lucy's father returned to his gardening.

Tim and Jack smiled at each other. Lucy was always like this. Mr Tāmati called her the class story-weaver. He said she could weave a story out of thin air.

The boys continued their building, while Lucy

kept on with her topiary. She snipped a bit here and chopped a bit there. Some branches were thick and thorny and didn't want to budge into the shape of a shaggy dog. Some clipped easily and neatly into furry legs, pricked-up ears and a straggly tail. It wasn't long before the tree was beginning to look a bit like Edmund: a shaggy old dog.

When Lucy had finished, her stomach was grumbling. "I'm going in to make some lunch," she called to her father.

"Okay, Luce. On your way, could you please get the mail from the letterbox?" her dad asked. "I'll see you inside soon."

"Yes, sir."

Tim and Jack, busy nailing planks of wood onto Tim's tangelo tree, looked at each other and smiled. "What about when she says, 'Yes, your Highness' when Mr Tāmati calls the roll," Jack said.

"I reckon Mr Tāmati thinks it's funny too," Tim said. "Y'know how he does that sort of smile?"

Out at the letterbox, Lucy noticed Ella across the road pumping up her bike tyre. "Got a flattie, Ella?" she called.

"Yeah. Dad thinks it's a puncture."

"Bummer. Hey, guess what? I've been doing topiary."

"What?"

"Topiary. On a bush. Come over and I'll show you." Lucy started to turn away, then looked back. "Come for lunch – we could have a picnic. Also, a princess might be visiting soon, so you can help me get everything ready for her."

"A princess?"

"Yeah."

"To your house?"

"Yeah. To see the topiary."

Ella simply nodded. She was used to Lucy's wild imagination. "I just need to let Serena know. Wait there." She ran inside to tell her stepmother that she was going to Lucy's for lunch.

From the tree next door, Tim and Jack could see the picnic preparations, so Lucy invited them to join in. Jack nipped home first to tell his mum.

The four friends sat on a rug under a tree, eating and discussing Lucy's shaggy dog topiary.

"I've got scratches all over my arms from it," Lucy said.

"It's harder than I thought it'd be to build a tree hut, too," Jack said, a piece of lettuce straggling from his lips.

"Ew, Jack, that's gross," Ella said. "Don't talk with your mouth full."

"Sorry," Jack apologised, swallowing loudly. "Anyway, problem is the nails. They keep bending, eh Tim?"

"Yeah, they're a bit blunt."

"You guys could finish your tree hut another day and help me get ready for the princess's visit today," Lucy suggested, "cos I've already thought of one problem. I haven't got a red carpet for the princess to walk on when she arrives. Royalty always walks on red carpets."

"So do movie stars," Tim said. "I saw the preview of the new Spiderman movie on the news and the actors were walking on a red carpet."

"Lucy, a princess isn't going to visit," Ella said gently. "It's just a story you're making up."

"Actually, a princess probably will visit, Ella, but if you guys don't want to help, then I can find some red carpet myself."

Ella sighed, rolling her eyes at Tim and Jack. "Gemma's got a red lavalava," she said. "I know that's not exactly a carpet, but there are massive flowers all over it. A princess would probably like it and it is red."

"Hmmm. That'd probably be all right," Lucy said, nodding. "I'm gonna phone Mum at work and ask if we can use her special tea set. Anyone got something special to eat at home?"

"Mum made a chocolate cake last night," Jack said. "It was for us to eat today anyway."

"Tea and cake," Lucy said. "Perfect."

After lunch, Lucy smoothed the red lavalava along the footpath in front of their house, ready for the princess's arrival. When neighbours passed, they asked what was going on. Some of them sniggered when Lucy told them. Others nodded politely, but Lucy could tell they thought she was just playing.

Lucy's father came out of the front door and called up to her on the footpath. "Luce, why don't you put the lavalava in the back yard instead?"

"Her private helicopter can't land in our back yard, Dad," Lucy called back. "Tui Street will have to be the helipad."

Shaking his head, her father went back inside. He didn't like to see her being made fun of.

The Tui Street kids stayed near the red carpet though. Terri juggled her soccer ball, and Gemma and Harry skateboarded down the footpath while Louie watched them, admiring their ollies and kick flips. Cloudbird perched on a branch nearby.

Meanwhile, Jack, Tim and Ella were arranging fold-up chairs around the picnic table in the back garden. They set out the teacups neatly beside the cake, which was beneath a special net cover that

Jack's mother had given them to keep flies away.

"You do know this princess is in her imagination," Ella said to the boys.

"Yeah, I know – we've all tried to tell her that," Jack replied.

"And even if there was a real princess," Ella said, "she might not like topiary."

Tim nodded. "And if someone *did* come, how would we know she was a real princess anyway? She could be pretending."

"True." Jack's eyebrows scrunched together worriedly. "I don't wanna share our chocolate cake with a liar."

"Guys, there is no princess!" Ella said. "It's just one of Lucy's stories. Anyway, there's a way to test whether someone's a real princess. You use a pea. Remember that fairy tale where they stuck a pea under a whole heap of mattresses and—" Ella stopped speaking. A distant hum was growing louder, and seemed to be getting closer. Then a roar filled the air, as if hundreds of lawnmowers had been switched on all at once.

Ella, Tim and Jack looked up. A helicopter was lowering in the sky, heading directly for Tui Street. The three friends' eyes widened.

"Is that her?" Ella shouted over the noise.

No one bothered to answer. Instead they began to run. They passed Lucy's dad, flinging the front door open and running onto the street with Tillie on his hip.

Beside the lavalava, they found Lucy, Terri, the twins and Louie staring up into the sky. At the entrance to Tui Street, a red helicopter descended slowly, hovering a few metres from the ground. As it grew closer, what had looked like a blob of yellow paint on both sides of the helicopter, turned out to be a large, sunny hibiscus flower. Edging slightly forward, the helicopter landed carefully beside the lavalava in front of Lucy's house.

Lucy turned to Ella, Jack and Tim and let out a long, joyous shriek.

"Hey!" Jack cried, his hands over his ears. "There's already enough noise!"

Lucy laughed. "It's just so … exciting!"

Neighbours came out of their houses, yelling to one another and making their way towards the lavalava.

The helicopter grew quiet and the rotors stopped spinning. The onlookers lowered their voices.

"Lucy was right," said Billie, the older girl who lived at number 10 Tui Street. "This must be the princess!"

"I wish I'd had a bit of notice," said Mrs McCarthy, from number 6. "I'd have dressed up a little."

"I wouldn't worry," said Mr Naufahu from number 11, stroking his grey beard. "She'll be too busy looking at Tillie and saying how cute she is to worry about what you're wearing." He turned to Lucy. "Royalty love babies."

Lucy looked at Tillie on her father's hip. She was pointing at the helicopter and repeating "haycop" over and over.

"Dad, do you think the princess will think Tillie's cute?" Lucy asked.

"Probably," her dad replied. "It'd be hard not to." He smiled down at Tillie and nodded. "Yes, it's a helicopter," he said to her. Looking back at Lucy, he added, "She might use more princessy words though, such as 'precious', or 'such a treasure', or 'utterly adorable'."

The door of the helicopter opened. A loud gasp and cheer greeted the princess. She was tall with wide shoulders and seemed young, possibly still a teenager. On top of her swirling black hair sat a crown that sparkled under the sun. She wore a long blue dress with tiny cream frangipani flowers dotted all over it. Her smile widened at the sight of the red lavalava ahead of her. As she stepped down to make her way along it, she nodded at people, greeting them politely. The crowd stepped back to make way for her. No one made a sound, not even Tillie, who usually made lots of noise.

When Mrs Gardner from number 9 held her baby out to the princess, Lucy heard her say, "How precious, what a wee treasure."

Finally, she stopped in front of Lucy. "Are you Lucy?" she asked, in a clear, bright voice, exactly the way Lucy expected a princess might speak.

"Yes, Your Highness, and this is my dad and my little sister, Tillie," Lucy replied.

"Oh, what a sweetheart, she's as sweet as a ripe mango," the princess said, reaching over to tickle Tillie under the chin. Then she turned to Lucy. "I hear you've been doing some topiary. I've come to see your shaggy dog tree. Would you show me?"

"Yes," Lucy replied. "Follow me, Your Highness." Proudly, she led the princess around to the back yard, while her dad went inside to put the kettle on.

Tim, Ella and Jack examined the princess closely as they followed behind.

"She has a crown and her own helicopter," Ella said. "She must be a real princess."

Tim shook his head. "Anyone can own a helicopter."

"Yeah, but you have to be mega-rich to own one, Tim, and princesses are rich," Jack said. "I reckon she's a princess."

"What if she hired it?" Tim asked.

"But that's expensive too, cos she'd also have to hire a pilot."

"Maybe we should look at the facts, Jack," Tim suggested. "Lucy's our friend. We need to make sure she's not being lied to."

Jack sighed. "Okay, but we have to be quick. I don't want to miss out on cake." He stopped walking and turned to Tim and Ella. "Fact one: royalty likes topiary. Fact two: she came in a helicopter, which means she could be a princess, because princesses are rich."

Tim scratched his head. "They're not exactly facts though, Jack. They're *clues* that she *could* be a princess."

Jack nodded. "Okay, so we have two clues."

"Another clue," Ella said, "is the crown she wears – it doesn't look like it's from the Two Dollar Shop."

"So," Jack said, "that's three clues. Anything else?"

Tim shook his head. "No, but we need evidence. Clues aren't good enough. We need proof."

Ella nodded, her serious face frowning slightly as she spoke. "I think Lucy deserves to know the truth.

In fact, we all do. The whole street does."

"We could try your pea idea, Ella," Tim suggested. "How does that work?"

"It's a fairy tale, Tim," Jack said.

Ignoring Jack, Tim asked, "So what do we have to do with the pea?"

"The princess felt a pea under lots of mattresses. It was proof that she was a real princess, because princesses are extra sensitive."

"We've got peas in our garden," Tim said.

"We've got peas in our freezer," Ella added. "But they're probably not so good. They'll thaw out and go mushy."

"You go and get a pea from your garden, Tim," Jack said. "Ella and I will keep an eye on things till you get back."

"And eat some cake, Jack?" Tim teased.

"Timbo, if everyone's eating cake, I'll have to join them. Would be rude not to." He grinned.

The pea vines in Tim's garden clung to the bamboo structure his dad had built. The pods weighed heavily, but the vines managed to stay upright and strong, like wire. Tim wondered how gravity didn't win, how those pods of fresh, crunchy peas didn't just pull the whole vine down. Carefully, he took a bulging pod in his hand, snapped it from the vine and slit it open with his fingernail. The peas inside were in a neat line. He liked their organisation. It was satisfying, like when dominoes fell perfectly or screwdrivers fitted screws exactly. Tim plucked the biggest, roundest pea from its pod. Rolling it between his thumb and forefinger, he shook his head. He doubted whether a princess would be able to feel the pea under a mattress. Quickly, he placed the pea in his shorts pocket and hurried back over the fence to join the royal tea party.

As Tim approached the small group in Lucy's back garden, he saw the princess standing in front of the shaggy dog tree. Sighing with pleasure, she ran her fingers gently over the bushy ears and said, "This tree is adorable." Reaching down to caress the twiggy paws, she murmured, "I'm so glad I came. It was worth the trip."

"I'm glad you came too," Lucy said.

The princess smiled at Lucy. "Meeting you and your friends and family has been rather special, Lucy. Maybe one day you could all come to see our topiary at the palace."

"Would you like a cup of tea, Your Highness?" Lucy's father asked. He set the steaming teapot down beside the cups and chocolate cake on the table under the tree.

"Oh, yes please," the princess replied. "Although, would you mind if I sat in the hammock? It's such a long time since I've sat in one."

"Not at all. Make yourself at home," Lucy's dad replied.

At that, the princess slipped off her shoes and sat back in the hammock, swaying gently. "Oh, it is good to have a little swing every now and then," she said. "Would it be too much trouble for me to have a cushion to pop under my shoulders, so I can sit up a little more to drink my tea?"

"I'll get one," Ella offered.

"Thanks, Ella. Get a large one off the sofa," Lucy's father said.

When Ella reappeared with a cushion almost as large as herself, she deliberately passed Tim on her way to the hammock. "Put the pea under this," she whispered out the corner of her mouth. Then loudly she said, "Here you are, Your Highness. This one looked the most comfortable."

The princess smiled and sat forward. "Oh lovely. Thank you so much."

Lucy lifted the large cushion on to the hammock behind the princess.

"Let me help." Tim stepped forward. Quickly, he took the pea from his pocket and wedged it beneath

199

the cushion that he and Ella positioned neatly behind the princess's back.

"Aren't you kind?" the princess said. "Now please, everyone, do have some tea and cake. I've held you up long enough."

Lucy's father passed a cup of tea and a slice of cake to the princess. Then he passed cake and juice to the children.

As they ate, Tim watched the princess closely. She had wriggled slightly, but seemed to be concentrating on the cake now. "This cake is absolutely delicious. Who iced it?" she asked, gently dabbing the corners of her mouth with a napkin.

"I did," Jack said. "Mum always lets me do the icing and then I get to lick the bowl and the spoon."

"You lick the bowl and spoon!" The princess's dark brown eyes were wide with disbelief. "Your mother lets you do that?"

"Yep." Jack was trying not to talk with his mouth full, but it meant he couldn't take another bite until the princess had stopped talking to him. He'd just have to wait.

"Sometimes the kitchen staff let me have the odd quick lick of the spoon, but I've never licked the bowl. Maybe I'll do that next time." She giggled and the sing-song sound dangled so mischievously between her and the children that it was impossible not to join in.

"Where are you from?" Lucy asked.

"Actually, it's not too far from here," the princess answered. "It's a small island. Only took a couple of hours to get here. I was very lucky that my parents are visiting Samoa by cruise ship, so the helicopter wasn't being used today."

Tim noticed the princess wriggle a little more. She leant forward and placed her hand on top of the cushion behind her.

"Are you okay, Princess?" Lucy asked.

"Yes, fine. It's just … there's something …"

"Here, let me help. I'll take your cup and saucer." Lucy took the dishes from the princess and placed them back on the table.

The princess twisted around and lifted the cushion, patting underneath it. "Ah, that's it. There's the little culprit." She held up the pea.

"A pea?" Lucy's dad asked. "How did a pea end up there? We don't have any in our vege garden."

The princess smiled. "Never mind how. It's fresh and it's my favourite vegetable." She opened her mouth and popped the pea inside, munching happily.

Tim, Jack and Ella looked at each other with

surprise. That was not what they'd expected!

After a little bit more hammock-swinging, tea-drinking and cake-eating, the princess stood up and brushed the crumbs off her long, flowing dress. "I really must go. I have to get to Samoa by supper time to attend a ball with the Prime Minister. My parents are expecting me there." Putting her shoes back on, she turned to Lucy, "I will never forget this day and I will always remember your topiary tree, Lucy, and your cake, Jack, and this hammock," she said.

"She ate the evidence!" Tim whispered.

"But she could feel it," Jack said quietly. "She's definitely a princess."

"True," Tim muttered. "But who does that? Eating something that could have been dropped by a bird or spat out of Tillie's mouth?"

"Ahh!" Jack clapped Tim playfully on the back. "You would have washed it first, wouldn't you, Tim?"

Tim smiled. His cheeks reddened. "It just wasn't very hygienic!"

Ella and Jack laughed quietly; Tim couldn't help but join in. Their laughter was soon drowned out by the sound of an advancing helicopter.

The princess, who'd just been tickling Tillie under the chin, looked up. "Paparazzi!" she cried.

"Paparazzi!" Lucy's dad exclaimed. "Why?"

"Please don't tell them I'm a princess!" the princess shrieked. "They'll never leave me alone!"

"Of course we won't," Lucy's father said. "Quick. Let's get you on your helicopter."

As they ran up the driveway, a car swung into it. More cars were parked up the road. Doors opened and slammed. Photographers, TV crews and newspaper reporters pushed and shoved past each other in their battle to get to the princess.

"Are you a real princess?" some of them yelled. The questions were coming so fast, they were difficult to hear properly: "Princess, where are you from?" "Who are your parents?" "Why did you come to Tui Street?" "Are you planning to meet with the Prime Minister?" "What do you think of New Zealand?" "Do you plan to look around while you're here?"

Lucy's father quickly closed the driveway gate. "Sorry, this is private property," he said. "Kids, Princess – quick, follow me!"

In the back yard, Lucy's dad quietly issued urgent orders. "Princess, crawl through the hole in the hedge into Tim's back yard. Lucy, you go with her. Tim and Jack, we need you up high somewhere, so you can keep lookout."

"The new tree hut?" Jack suggested, pointing at their half-built tree hut next door.

"It'd be a good observation tower," Tim said.

"Perfect," Lucy's dad agreed.

"What about me?" Ella asked.

"Ella, you go up to the gate and distract the reporters. Get them to look at Terri. She's doing soccer tricks on the street. The twins are on their skateboard ramp too. Tell them about Louie and his tame tui. Get them interested in something else. Think you can do that?"

Ella nodded.

"Good. Tim and Jack, when Ella has distracted them, tell the princess to run to the helicopter. Wait till no one is looking this way, though, or she'll be swamped – crushed by that crowd."

The black press helicopter circled the bottom of Tui Street, rattling the seven letterboxes next to Terri's house as it passed over them. Swooping back over Lucy's house, a woman on a loudspeaker called to them from its open door. "Is she a real princess? Wave to us if she's a real princess."

"I'm going to turn the waterblaster on this helicopter if it swoops down again," Lucy's father said. "While I do that, Lucy – you, Jack and Tim race through the hole in the hedge with the princess. Lucy, stay with her till you see her safely on her helicopter."

Lucy's father walked over to the hose reel. With Tillie still on his hip, he connected up the waterblaster and turned it on. The woman in the black helicopter leant out of the open door, calling to them. The helicopter lowered further. Wind from the propeller blew the hammock up and down, like a boat tossed in waves. Lucy's dad aimed the nozzle of the waterblaster. The water arced upwards in one powerful torrent, surging through the open door of the helicopter. The woman leapt backwards. "Hey, what—?" she yelled, but the water drowned her out and she quickly shut the door as the pilot turned the helicopter away.

"Run, Princess, run now!" Lucy's father called, still unleashing water on the retreating helicopter. "You go too, kids. I've got this covered."

Tim, Jack and Lucy ran to the hole in the hedge. Politely, they stood back and let the princess go first. She crawled on her hands and knees through the muddy grass to Tim's house, Lucy following. Tim and Jack scrabbled through and climbed up to the half-built tree hut, while Lucy and the princess crawled under the deck, out of sight.

"Oh no, your dress is getting ruined!" Lucy said, trying to brush twigs and mud from the princess's sleeve.

"Never mind that," the princess said. "I'm more worried about that dog. It won't bark at us, will it? I'd hate it to give our hiding place away."

"What dog?" Lucy said, peering out from under the deck.

It was Edmund. He'd wandered over from Jack's house and was making his way to the hole in the hedge.

"He's going to my place," Lucy said. "Wonder why?"

Up at the front gate, Ella loudly directed people's attention to Terri and the twins. She proudly explained that Terri was so good at soccer, she'd been picked to trial for the national Girls' Under-15 team. "And, on your way down the street, you'll notice the twins' house on the left. They do amazing tricks on their skateboard ramp. And on the right at number eight, Louie has a tame tui. That's definitely worth a look."

It was working. Some reporters were jotting down what Ella had said and making their way along the street to have a look.

Unfortunately, half of the reporters stayed put, questioning Ella or speaking loudly into cell phones and pushing against the gate.

"It's all over Twitter now," one reporter said,

hooking her long blonde hair back with her sunglasses, phone pinned to her ear. "There's no point in hiding her."

"And Instagram's buzzing with photos of her," another reporter said. "You might as well let us at her. We just want an interview."

Ella could feel the gate creaking as the reporters leant against it.

"There could be some money in this for you too," a young man said, "if you agree to let us in." He leant hard on the gate, his breath hot and sour in Ella's face.

The gate made a cracking sound. Ella stepped back nervously. "Be careful!" she said.

The reporters kept pushing against the gate and, with one almighty crack, the bolt broke off, pulling a plank of wood with it. The throng of reporters surged through and Ella leapt aside, frightened she might be knocked down. In a mad frenzy, the reporters ran through to the back yard. Some ran onto the deck and through the house. Others ran down to the creek. One reporter, with sunglasses so dark he could barely see, fell in, only to find himself being filmed by a TV crew. "Turn off your cameras!" he yelled angrily, as he adjusted his glasses and clambered up the bank.

There were two paparazzi helicopters now. Lucy's dad alternated the waterblaster from one to the other, while Tillie squealed with delight.

Then an older man with a microphone slowed as he walked beside the shaggy dog tree. He stopped, looked at the tree, and leant in to listen. "Be quiet, everyone!" he yelled. "Listen to this! Come and listen."

The reporters nearby stopped looking for the princess and made their way to the shaggy dog tree. "Shhh!" they said to each other.

The shaggy dog tree seemed to be barking. Little yelping barks came from within the belly of the shaggy dog topiary.

"Is it really barking?" one woman asked. "It's a bush!"

"Listen for yourself!" the older man said. "We're not imagining it, are we?"

"Let's film this," a young man said. "This is going to make great news. A topiary bush that barks!"

Another reporter turned to Ella. "When did you notice that this bush could bark?" she asked.

While the reporters marvelled at the barking bush, Jack and Tim observed from the half-built tree hut.

"The reporters are still filming Terri," Jack said.

"And some are interviewing Gemma and Harry

on the skateboard ramp," Tim added.

"Louie's showing Cloudbird to a few too." Jack looked at Tim. "Might be safe to let the princess run for it now," Jack said.

Tim nodded. He looked down at Lucy and the princess, peering out from under the deck. He gave them a 'thumbs up' sign. "GO!"

The princess crawled out first, Lucy behind her. She ran up the side of Tim's house, around to the front and up the garden path. Without a word, Lucy followed her. At Tim's gate, they could see the reporters further down Tui Street interviewing the twins and filming Terri. Behind them, they could hear the drone of the press helicopters and Edmund barking.

"Run, Princess," Lucy whispered loudly. "Run!"

The princess kicked off her shoes and sprinted up the footpath, holding her torn, muddy dress up so she wouldn't trip. She ran over the red lavalava and clambered into the helicopter. As the door closed behind her, Tim noticed for the first time a name signwritten on it: Princess Teuila.

"There she is!" someone yelled.

"It's the princess," another person called. "She's escaping!"

"Lucy!" the princess called down to her. "Thank you. I'll never forget you or your friends or your—"

"We won't forget you either!" Lucy yelled. "Now please go!"

"Goodbye, Lucy!" the princess called, as they closed the door.

"Bye, Princess!" Lucy yelled.

The door clicked shut. The throng of reporters running towards the helicopter stopped. The helicopter's twin engines roared into action. The crowds separated, stepping back out of the way of the spinning rotor blades. Reporters talked loudly, yelling over the noise, speaking animatedly into cameras.

Amidst the crowds of people, Jack, Tim, Ella, Lucy, her father and Tillie stood on the footpath watching the helicopter edge down the street. Rising upwards, it swooped over Terri with her soccer ball and Harry and Gemma on their skateboard ramp. Circling, it soared up over Tui Street, past the crowds, past Louie with Cloudbird nearby, until it was only a small dot in the distance.

The people gathered outside Lucy's house began to make their way back to their homes. Reporters returned to their cars. The black press helicopters soared up and away.

Terri, Gemma and Harry walked up to join their friends.

"We're gonna be on TV tonight," Terri said. "Those reporters filmed me practising soccer skills."

"Yeah and us on our skateboard ramp," Gemma added.

"Looks like our plans worked then," Lucy's father said. Lucy nodded. She felt pleased for the princess, but sad that she'd gone. Her dad squeezed her hand. "Come on," he said. "I think your friends deserve cake."

"And Edmund deserves a bone," Ella added. "He's the cleverest dog I've ever met."

"Those reporters really thought the shaggy dog tree was barking?" Jack said with a chuckle.

Everybody laughed.

"That'll be on the news tonight too," Tim said. "They filmed the barking bush!"

Later, the hose lay in a tangle under the shaggy dog tree. The hammock hung, twisted and torn. The street was silent now, except for the sound of hammering as Lucy's father fixed his gate. The Tui Street kids had finished the cake. It had been a long day and it was time for everyone to head home.

Jack, Tim and Ella were the last to leave. As they walked up Lucy's driveway, Tim saw the lavalava still lying on the footpath.

"Hey, the red carpet," he said. "You'd better give that back to Gemma."

Ella picked it up and shook it out. She draped it over her shoulder and around her head, like a movie star. "Do I look like a princess now?" she asked.

"Nah," Tim said.

"Hmmm," Jack said. "Let's look at the facts ..."

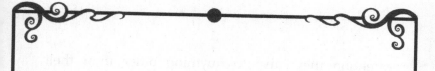

The Seven at the Bottom of the Street

TERRI LIVED AT THE BOTTOM of Tui Street. Her favourite pastime was practising soccer skills with the other Tui Street kids. Many afternoons were spent doing juggles, tackles, kicks and dribbles on a long driveway at number fourteen, right next door to Terri's house. Although the friends practised there regularly, they hadn't taken much notice of the seven small letterboxes that sat in a neat row at the top of the driveway. In fact, the only

attention they gave to anything other than their soccer practice was Terri's dog, Chelsea (named after the English football club). Chelsea mostly sat beside the letterboxes, keeping a loyal eye on Terri, but being a golden retriever, she sometimes felt the need to fetch the ball. She was slowly learning that, if she left the ball alone she would receive hugs and pats from the Tui Street kids, rather than the frustrated yells and orders to go home that she was subjected to if she interfered with the game.

One day, when Terri, Jack and Tim were kicking the ball around, Terri did one of her extreme kicks, hitting one of the knee-high letterboxes so hard that it bent backwards.

"Oh no!" Terri yelled, running up to the boys, who were inspecting the damage. "It's totally bent over. I don't believe it!"

"I do. You kick like a pro," Jack said. Terri kicked better than anyone else he knew, even though she was the shortest in his class.

"A pro would aim better," Terri said dismally. She looked at the bent letterbox, then at the other six letterboxes, still standing straight. Her eyes flicked to Chelsea for a moment and then back to the letterboxes. "These letterboxes are exactly the same height as Chelsea," she said. "Why would they be so low? Even I have to bend down to reach them."

"Ever met who lives down there?" Jack asked, gazing down the length of the driveway.

Terri shrugged. "Sort of. They leave early in the mornings so I only see them when they come home in those big vans. They always wave at us. Seem nice." Terri picked up the ball. "I'm gonna have to pay to fix the letterbox. Mum and Dad won't be pleased – they've just paid my fees for squad training."

Terri had been chosen to trial for the national Girls' Under-15 team. She would train over the summer with the group and then, if she was chosen, she'd go to the international tournament in Japan. She would be the youngest girl in the team at only twelve years old.

"You could pretend you didn't do it. We could just say we found it like that," Jack suggested.

"Jack, she'll feel bad if she does that," Tim said. Looking at Terri, he added, "You will feel bad, Terri."

"Yeah, you probably will," Jack agreed.

"I'll leave a note for them," Terri said. "I'll stick it in the letterbox. Better go and get some paper and tell Mum. Don't be surprised if you hear her yelling from here." Terri gave a small smile, threw the ball up, caught it on her head and balanced it there, avoiding her short blonde ponytail as she moved backwards and forwards to keep it from falling. "Come on, Chelsea. See ya, guys!"

Terri's mother didn't yell. She did purse her lips for a brief moment though. "Oh well. It's done now. No point agonising over it. We'll just have to fix it. A note's a good idea."

"Do you know their names, Mum? Who shall I write the note to?"

"No, I don't know any names. I've met a couple of them before, but I'm hopeless at remembering names. I know that there are seven units down that drive. They were built by the council for people with disabilities. Hurry up with that note though. Dad's dropping you to squad training tonight and he won't want to muck around. You know Dad."

"I'll be quick." Terri tore a piece of paper from the notepad beside the phone. She wrote:

Hello. I bent your letterbox by mistake, playing soccer. Sorry. Let me know if you want us to get it fixed or give you the money for it. Thanks.
From your neighbour Terri, at number 12.

Folding the note in half, she ran out the front door.

The letterboxes were numbered 14A to 14G. Terri stuffed the note into the bent letterbox, and ran home to get ready for training.

Squad training wasn't easy. The other girls were so much older – and bigger – than she was. Most of them were friendly and chatted with her a bit. Some were extra nice, like Hera, who sat beside Terri and shared some biscuits before training started. There was one girl though, Antonia, who had never spoken to Terri, and didn't even look at her. Worst of all, she never passed the ball to Terri when they split into teams for practice games. She just didn't seem to see her.

That evening, Terri's dad mentioned it for the first time on the way home from squad training. "That tall girl, Antonia – she never passes to you."

"I know." Terri leaned forward and switched radio stations.

"Oi, I was enjoying that! Old love songs are the best."

"Dad, they are not! And then you start singing along, so this is double ear protection."

"Better than this hiphop, rappy stuff – it hurts my ears." They were at the traffic lights, sitting in rows of cars, lights beaming into the busy darkness. "Don't let her get to you, Terri-girl," her father said quietly.

"I won't." It was hard though. Whenever Terri yelled, "Over here! I'm here!" Antonia ignored her and kicked to anyone else but her.

The note Terri found in her letterbox next day was in small, neat writing:

> Hi Terri. Don't worry about it. We can fix it ourselves.
> We would like to ask a favour of you though. Could
> you drop in on Saturday afternoon sometime?
> We'll explain then. Thanks for your honesty.
> From the seven of us at number 14.

"Wonder what they want," Terri mused to Jack and Tim later. She was sitting on the stone wall outside her house finishing an apple, while the boys kicked the ball around.

"Maybe they want you to pick up toys or sweep up leaves," Jack said. "That's what Mum and Dad get me to do. Then they tell me I'm doing them a favour and I say 'but you told me I had to do it, so it's not really a favour'." Jack kicked the ball to Tim.

"Want us to come with you on Saturday?" Tim asked, kicking the ball back. "I've always wanted to see who lives down there."

"Mum jokes that the seven dwarfs live there," Jack

said. "If I'm grumpy, she tells me I'm in the wrong house!"

Terri smiled. Jack's mother could be funny sometimes. "Yeah, you guys come with me on Saturday. If they are the seven dwarfs, they might think I'm Snow White and make me be their housekeeper."

"You'd be cooking and cleaning for them for the rest of your life," Jack said.

"Who'd want to do that? That's *so* not a happy ending." Terri spat out an apple pip.

"The happy ending is when the prince kisses her and she wakes up," Tim explained.

"Ew! Who wants someone they've never met before to kiss them? Might be a warty, old, hairy guy. Imagine waking up to that!"

Jack and Tim laughed.

"I'd rather someone woke me up with an ice cream." Terri threw the apple core into a nearby bush. "Or a soccer ball." She jumped off the wall, tackled the ball off Jack and dodged past Tim, dribbling it towards the seven letterboxes. "Come on, let's practise on their driveway."

It was summer. The afternoon was warm and the cicadas sounded like croaky old men. The three friends juggled, tackled, kicked and dribbled as if soccer were the most important thing in the world. For Terri, it was.

Although they'd played soccer on the driveway many times, they'd never actually ventured to the bottom, where it forked. To the left were three small, brick units connected to each other. To the right were four that looked exactly the same. Each unit had a ramp leading up to the front door.

"You could skateboard straight out of the house down those ramps," Jack said when they returned on Saturday.

"Let's ask if we can bring our skateboards down here some time," Terri suggested.

The door handle of 14A was very low, perfect for Terri's height. She reached out and pressed the doorbell. From inside, they heard the sound of a soft motor approaching. The door was pulled open slowly, and someone within said, "Hi."

The children couldn't see who had spoken until a young man in a wheelchair appeared, gently rolling towards them. "Sorry, here I am. I just had to whizz backwards a bit to open the door." His blonde hair was swept up into a ponytail. He had a tattoo of a surfboard on his left upper arm and his T-shirt had a picture of a beach and the word 'Hawaii' on it. He wore faded jeans that were too loose on his thin legs, as if his legs had begun to fade too.

"Hi, I'm Chris," he said, reaching out to shake Terri's hand. They were the same height. "You must be our neighbour. It's Terri, right?"

"Yeah." She shook his hand. "And this is Jack and Tim."

Chris smiled. "We've seen you guys playing soccer." He shook hands with the boys. "I'll just tell the others you're here. Come on in and have a seat." Reversing his wheelchair, he pressed a button on a gadget stuck to the wall beside the front door. Leaning into the gadget, he spoke loudly, "Hey everyone, they're here."

Terri, Tim and Jack sat down beside each other on the sofa, the only seat in the small lounge room.

"That's an intercom so that we can talk to each other. They're on their way over now," Chris explained, wheeling over towards them. "Would you guys like a drink? I've got homemade lemonade. My caregiver makes it. The lemons are from our tree out the back."

"No thank you," all three answered at once.

"Wow, how did you do that? I mean … are you, like, three bodies connected to one mind?" Chris smiled.

Jack answered, "Yep, I'm the mind and they just do as I say."

"Yeah, right," Terri said, nudging Jack.

Chris laughed. "Hey, did you notice I fixed the letterbox? Pretty easy really – I just welded a new steel pole onto it. I'm a welder by trade. Ah, here they are."

The sound of chatter and laughter filled the room as three men and three women wheeled in through the front door. The room filled quickly. That explained the lack of furniture, Terri thought.

"Okay, this is Lily, Sula, Jason, Bella, Brett and Kepa," Chris said. "Guys, this is Terri, Jack and Tim."

Everyone greeted each other cheerfully, except for Jason, whose 'Hi' was only just audible. He was younger than the rest. Tim wondered if he was still a teenager.

Once the greetings were over, Chris spoke again. "When you wrote that you'd knocked the letterbox over playing soccer, we couldn't believe our luck. It was like it was meant to happen."

Terri, Jack and Tim looked at each other. How could breaking Chris's letterbox be good luck?

Seeing their confusion, Sula began to speak. Her dark brown eyes shifted from one child to the next. She leant forward, tossing her long plaits behind her. "We need to learn how to play soccer. We want to enter a wheelchair soccer tournament."

"We want to win it," said the small girl with short, pink-streaked, blonde hair. "We're entering to win."

"You're so competitive, Lily!" Kepa said, laughing. "She tries to beat us at everything – like wheelchair races." His thick, long plait didn't flick around like Sula's did. Instead, it sat solidly between his thick shoulders.

"We need your help with soccer tactics. We know the rules are a bit different in wheelchair soccer, but … what do you think?" Sula continued.

"You need eleven in a soccer team," Tim said.

"This is wheelchair soccer," Bella explained, "so there are only six players in a team. We'll have one sub, which we'll need. It's played indoors cos wheelchairs don't work so well on grass. We're going to call our team, 'The Seven'."

Bella was tall. Even in her wheelchair, she seemed to tower over the others. Her face, her arms, her red hair were all long. Terri wondered how it was that some people were so tall. Her mum told her there was no point in wishing she was taller and her dad always said that good things come in small packages. Still, sometimes being short wasn't easy, especially at squad training, where the difference in age was already noticeable enough.

"So, will you?" Brett asked, peering over the glasses on his long nose.

With a jolt, Terri realised they were waiting for her to say something. "Will I ...?"

"Be our coach."

Terri felt a little uncomfortable at the idea. They were a lot older than she was. It would feel strange telling them what to do.

"What do you think?" Chris asked.

"I do owe you a favour, I guess," Terri replied. At least the favour was related to soccer. She'd been worried they were going to ask her to weed their garden or mow their lawns.

"You'll need to read up on the rules for wheelchair soccer. They're a bit different," Brett said.

"I can do that," Terri answered. "I like looking up stuff on the internet."

"Great. First practice next Saturday afternoon?" Chis asked.

"Yip, that's a good time, cos my games are in the morning."

Chris slapped his hands on his legs. "Next Saturday then, two o'clock, in our driveway." Terri nodded. Chris reached out and shook her hand. "It's a deal."

The field was dry. Any last drops of moisture had been sucked up greedily by the sun. The girls' soccer boots pounded heavily on the thirsty, brittle grass. The squad had been divided into three lines and each line dribbled the ball around cones set in zigzags. As Terri dribbled the ball, she memorised the activities they'd done so far, so that she could try and use them when she coached The Seven on Saturday afternoon.

From the opposite direction, Antonia dribbled around the cones parallel to Terri's cones. As she passed Terri, she leant in slightly. "Dwarf!" she muttered. Terri, focusing intently on dribbling, looked up immediately, but Antonia had gone past. Looking behind, she could see Antonia laughing loudly with another girl.

Later, their coach split them into two teams to play against each other. This was Terri's favourite part of training: the game. The thrill of running, tackling, possessing the ball was so good, that often Terri lay in bed visualising it before she went to sleep. This evening, Terri had tackled the ball from the opposition a number of times. After one particularly good tackle, just as Terri was turning the ball to pass to someone, Antonia's voice drifted like a thin wisp of smoke from her left: "Midget."

Just loud enough for Terri to hear.

Terri's brain seemed to stop. Her legs felt numb. Antonia swooped in from her left, tackled the ball from her, turned and ran with it towards her goal.

Later, as Terri sat on the grass wrestling her boots off and guzzling thirstily from her water bottle, Hera said, "I heard what she said to you."

"It's okay," Terri said.

"No it's not. Don't let her get to you. She deliberately threw you off course to get the ball off you."

"Why doesn't she like me?"

Hera shrugged. "Wait till you meet her mother. She's worse. She thinks her daughter plays better than everyone. No one is better than her precious Antonia."

"Doesn't sound nice."

"She's not. No wonder Antonia's like she is."

When Saturday came, Terri, Tim and Jack used buckets and ice cream containers instead of cones and left bigger spaces between them so that the wheelchairs could manoeuvre around them.

Chelsea, Terri's dog, sat in her usual place by the letterboxes.

"Okay, so in wheelchair soccer, they play twenty-five minutes each half," Terri explained. "They dribble or kick the ball with their foot if they can, but if they can't, they use their wheelchair or hands, so it's kind of like basketball-soccer. The thing is, they're not allowed to hold the ball for more than five seconds, so they can't just carry the ball on their lap and race around in their wheelchairs."

"I read that players can use electric wheelchairs or manual ones," Tim added. "Do you think that's fair?"

"Well, if you can't use your arms to push yourself, you don't have a choice, do you?" Terri answered. "Some people can't use their fingers to press buttons on the electric wheelchair, so they're allowed a person to push them. The pusher can't get involved in the game though. They just do what the person in the wheelchair tells them to do."

"How do they stop the ball from going under the wheelchair or getting stuck between the wheels?" Jack asked.

"Apparently, players sometimes stick a flat piece of wood or metal in front of their footrest, which they can use to help them pass the ball and kick goals. Stops the ball from going under their wheelchairs too," Tim explained.

Looking up, Terri saw The Seven coming up the driveway towards them. The sound of their chatter and laughter grew as they approached.

"That guy, Jason, doesn't say much," Tim said.

"Shhh. He'll hear you." Terri straightened up from pumping up a ball. She watched the seven neighbours advancing in their wheelchairs. She'd never seen a wheelchair soccer game until she'd watched one on YouTube yesterday. In fact, she'd never even heard of it before she met these people.

Terri began the training session with some stretches that her dad had suggested. She tried to explain each stretch carefully. "Firstly, we'll stretch our necks gently by slowly tilting our heads from side to side."

"What if your hair gets caught in your spokes?" Kepa asked. "Better watch out, Bella."

"It's in a ponytail, stupid!" Bella replied, shaking her ponytail from side to side to make it obvious.

"Still long enough to get caught in your wheel, though," Brett said, looking over his glasses at her and grinning. "It's a safety hazard. You should put it in a bun."

Bella straightened her head from the stretch and poked her tongue out at him. "Stop telling me what to do, Brett. My hair's fine how it is."

"Right," Tim interrupted, "let's try another stretch, Terri. How about arms?"

Terri sat in front of her maths homework at the kitchen table. It was a struggle to concentrate and she found herself wondering about Jason. He hadn't spoken much at the practice, apart from 'Hi' and 'Bye'. He was definitely the best soccer player of The Seven. He moved quickly and his arms were strong. Twice he'd managed to dribble the ball between the cones and fire it straight into the makeshift goal they'd made with wheelie bins.

Terri's mum interrupted her thoughts. "Hey, dreamy, there's a text for you from Hera." She put her phone down beside Terri.

Terri picked up her mother's mobile. She wasn't allowed a phone of her own yet, so she'd had to give the coach and team her mum's mobile number. All the other girls had their own phones. Terri felt her face redden just to think of it. She clicked to open up the text from Hera.

Terri, this is urgent. Check our team FB page. You should talk to Jules about this.

Talk to the coach about what? Terri would have to ask if she could go on the computer now. She wasn't allowed to go on Facebook much. Her parents had only let her join because the soccer coach insisted that everyone be able to communicate with each other through Facebook.

On the team page, Terri saw immediately why Hera had texted her. Antonia had posted: "Why do we have to play with a midget?"

Three people had commented underneath.

Hera had written, "Delete your post, Antonia."

Liana had written, "Don't be nasty. She's got heaps of talent."

Rose had written, "She's a good player. She'll probably get selected."

Terri minimised the screen then enlarged it again. Antonia's profile photo was a close-up of Antonia with a soccer ball balanced on her head like a crown. Terri clicked on it and there, stretching across Antonia's Facebook wall were the words, "Who's the greatest soccer player of us all?"

Quickly, Terri clicked back to the team page. Should she comment on Antonia's post? What would she write? 'Why don't you like me?' No, she couldn't do that. She stared at Antonia's question for a long time. 'Why do we have to play with a midget?'

Finally, Terri logged off and shut down the computer. She could see her own reflection in the dark computer screen, like a mirror. It was faint, but at least it was there. She did exist, much as Antonia may wish she didn't.

Terri had begun to wish that Antonia would just completely ignore her again, like she had in the very beginning. As soon as Terri arrived at squad training on Tuesday evening and sat down to put on her boots, Antonia plonked herself down on the grass, near enough for Terri to hear her. She sighed, took her phone out of her bag and looked at it for a few seconds. She began to speak to her phone, "Facebook, Facebook, what does everyone think about having a midget in our team?" Her eyes stayed fixed on her phone as if someone were truly answering her. "What? You mean other team members wish she wasn't here too?" She put her phone down and turned to Terri. "Did you hear that? It's not just me who feels that way about midgets."

Terri tried to think of something to say, but her brain had that slow feeling again, like a fog had descended. Before she could think of an answer, a car door slammed and a woman's voice called, "Antonia! You left your water bottle in the car. I had to drive back with it. Don't want you to be thirsty."

"Here, throw it, Mum!" Antonia called, standing up.

"No, I won't throw it. It might break." Antonia's mother walked from the car park to her daughter. From where she sat on the grass, Terri's eyes travelled upward from the designer boots to the designer jeans, tight tee shirt, red lipstick and black hair that sat in a neatly-cut bob. She was like one of those dolls – the ones that looked pretty in a bossy, controlling way. It would be hard to relax in her home.

"Here you go, sweetie." Antonia's mother passed her the water bottle. "Oh, who's this?" She looked over at Terri, a smile set firmly on her face. "You're someone I haven't seen before. What's your name?"

"I'm Terri."

"Oh yes, Antonia's mentioned you. I remember because Terri's a boy's name. That was all the fashion for a while. Girls were given names like Jamie and Stevie."

"No, no. My name's Teresa. Everyone calls me Terri, though."

Antonia's mother's smile peeled away a bit, like a tiny bit of wallpaper being picked at. "I'd never allow Antonia to be called Toni."

That confusing fog settled on Terri again. She had no idea how to reply to this. Antonia's mother continued to speak about squad training and how exciting it would be when the team was chosen. Then she left, her heels stabbing the hard ground, making neat little holes exactly the same distance from each other, as she walked away.

At the end of practice, coach Jules took Terri aside. She explained that she'd seen Antonia's post on their team Facebook page and she'd told her to delete it. She said it would not happen again and that Antonia was sorry she'd done it.

Terri nodded and said, "Thanks, Jules." She didn't know how to tell her that Antonia had just used the 'midget' word again that very evening.

"You're playing so well, Terri. You have a very high chance of being selected for the rep team," Jules said. "Keep it up!"

The following Saturday, The Seven practised at an indoor soccer venue that Chris had booked. The Seven travelled in mobility vans, especially designed for wheelchairs. Their seatbelts locked around parts of the wheelchair so that it couldn't roll. Jack, Tim and Terri travelled in the same large van as Jason.

After five minutes of chatting with Tim and Jack, Terri decided to try to involve Jason in their conversation. "Are you looking forward to the tournament, Jason?"

Jason nodded. "Yes."

"How old are you?" Jack asked.

"Eighteen."

The only time he answered with more than one

word, was when Tim asked him if he'd played soccer before. Jason's head lifted slightly. "Yeah. First Eleven at school. Mid-fielder."

"I play mid-field too," Terri said.

"Did you have an accident?" Jack asked.

"Yep."

"What kind of an accident?" Jack persevered, ignoring the nudge Tim gave him.

"Car accident. My fault. Took a corner too fast."

"Anyone else hurt?"

"Just a tree," Jason said. "But I'll never walk again. Won't play soccer either."

"Yes, you will," Terri said. "You're playing today."

Jason nodded. "True." He tapped his fingers on the arm of his wheelchair. He seemed uncomfortable, as if he wanted to say more, as if he'd worked out how to open a door, but he wasn't sure how to go through it. He took a deep breath and spoke, "My mother wants to film us and put it on Facebook. She's glad I'm playing soccer again, even if it's in a wheelchair."

"I hate Facebook," Terri said.

"Are you on Facebook?" Jack asked. "Mum says I'm not allowed until I'm thirteen."

"Yeah, but only because of squad training. I wish I didn't have to be on it."

"Why?" Jason asked. "Most kids want to be on it."

Terri looked down at her hands and shrugged. "I just don't like it, that's all."

The Seven were improving. Most evenings, they practised on their driveway. It was best to train on the indoor soccer courts though. The floor was perfect for wheelchairs. In fact, the wheelchairs glided so well that the players had to steer them carefully to avoid crashes.

Often Tim, Terri, Jack and the other Tui Street kids played against them to give them some game practice. One of the best things about this was the good-natured yelling from The Seven. They hurled insults at them and at each other.

"Hey, you cheat!"

"What was that? Ref! Ref!"

"That's not a pass!"

"Oi, get out of my way!"

Jason was the only one who never joined in with the friendly insults. One day, however, Terri realised Jason was smiling at some of the insults thrown at him as he whisked the ball away from someone and sped towards his goal, dribbling the ball with his hands. Jason, smiling! The tournament was only a month away and Terri could see that the team was working well together now. She felt a small twist in her stomach. If only it was this much fun at her squad training.

After practice one Saturday, on the way back in the van, Jason surprised them by starting a conversation. "You trialling for the national Under-15s, Terri?"

"Yeah." Terri tried to twist around from the passenger seat in the front, but she knew she shouldn't, because sometimes it made her carsick.

"That's pretty good for someone so young. How's it going?"

"Okay."

"Okay? Sounds as bad as Facebook."

Jack laughed. "Her name was called out at assembly when she got picked to trial."

"I love soccer and I love training," Terri said, "but … there's this girl …" Terri remembered the numb feeling in her head when Antonia called her a midget. "She's not very nice."

"How? Is she mean to you?" Tim asked.

Terri nodded.

"Why?" Tim asked. He couldn't imagine why someone wouldn't like Terri.

Terri shrugged.

"She's probably jealous," Jason said. "Bet she

wishes she was as good as you. You're probably better than she is, even though she's older."

Terri turned back to face the front, not because she was feeling carsick, but because a slow, hot tear was making its way down her cheek. From his wheelchair in the back, Jason said, "You've got nothing to be ashamed of, Terri. You haven't done anything wrong."

"I'll come and tell her to leave you alone," Jack said.

"Yeah," Tim said. "Me too."

Terri still couldn't speak. More tears ran down her cheeks. The taxi van driver passed her a small packet of tissues from the glove box.

The van stopped to let the kids out at the top of Jason's driveway. From where she sat, Terri could see the seven letterboxes.

"She'll sort it out, won't you, Terri?" Jason said. "If you can coach our crazy team, you can do anything!" There was a hint of a smile on his face.

Terri nodded and sniffed.

"I'm just down this driveway if you need me," Jason added.

"Thanks," Terri said, as she opened the van door and stepped down. "See you later." The van door shut quietly behind her.

At Tuesday squad training the following week, Terri found herself on the same team as Antonia in the practice game. She'd developed a habit of keeping a watchful eye on the older girl and carefully distancing herself whenever she came too close. It was particularly hard to do when they were on the same team. Antonia didn't pass to her at all. Terri continually called, "I'm here," and "I'm free," and "Over here," but to no avail. Antonia not only didn't pass to her, she frequently muttered "dwarf," "shorty" or "midget" under her breath when she was near. Somehow she managed to say these things out of the hearing of the other players.

At the end of practice, Jules reminded them that in a couple of weeks they'd be picking players for the team to go to the international Under-15 Girls' soccer tournament in Japan. Terri breathed in deeply. Wouldn't it be amazing to be in the team? Imagine playing girls' teams from all over the world. She felt her heart race to think of it. Slinging her boot bag over her shoulder, she began to make her way to the car where her dad waited, no doubt listening to some rubbishy old love songs.

With the cunning of a fox, Antonia seized her moment, slipped her phone out of her boot bag, gathered her belongings and walked briskly towards the carpark. Catching up with Terri, she whispered loudly, "You won't get picked, dwarfie." Looking at her phone, she said, "Oh look, it's Facebook. Tell us, Facebook, do midgets go to Japan? Hmmm. I thought so." She turned to Terri. "Looks like they don't!"

In the car, Terri's dad was humming to a love song. "Hey, hey, it's my soccer-girl!" he said, turning the music down slightly as she climbed in the car. "How was practice?"

Terri had no words. Her thoughts were stuck in a place where words like 'midget' and 'dwarf' pounded in her ears constantly.

"Everything okay?" her dad asked, starting the car.

Terri nodded slowly.

"That tall girl still not passing to you, huh? I've been watching for the last twenty minutes and she sure doesn't want you to show her up."

"What do you mean?" Terri asked.

"Terri, the more you have the ball, the more you get to show your skills. She doesn't want the coach seeing you do well all the time. She's scared she won't get picked."

Terri sat quietly listening to the songs of some old band singing about love.

"Would an ice cream help?"

Terri shook her head.

"How about you put the radio on your station?"

Terri shook her head again.

"How about you tell your coach what's going on?"

Terri looked out the window away from her dad. She needed to be by herself. She just needed to sit quietly with Chelsea until the hazy feeling melted away.

That evening, Terri's mother came into her bedroom just as she was finishing her homework. "Got a text from your coach. She wants you to check new practice times she's posted on Facebook. You can jump on the computer quickly now if you want to."

"Okay. Thanks." Terri pulled her feet out from under the dog, stood up and put her books in her bag. Chelsea stretched and stood up beside her.

Her mum stayed in the doorway. "You okay, sweet pea?"

"Mmm."

"Dad's been telling me about that girl at soccer. We can always ring her parents if this is becoming a problem."

Terri thought of Antonia's mother. Somehow she didn't think that would work. "It's okay, Mum. I'm okay. I'll quickly check Facebook now, then go to bed."

Along with the new practice times, there was a personal message waiting for her. Terri's finger hovered over the mouse. Did she want to read this message? What if it was from someone nice on the team though, like Hera or Liana? It was worth having a quick check. She clicked on the small message symbol. Antonia's profile picture and name sprang up before her eyes. Underneath, there were five words: "Dwarfs belong in the circus." Terri read it again. "Dwarfs belong in the circus." She shut down the computer. The words were gone. It was just her face now, reflected in the computer screen, mirroring her uncertainty with its blurred features and hazy edges.

Terri stood up. Her parents were watching TV in the lounge. She took her jacket off the hook by the front door. Chelsea was beside her, tail wagging excitedly. "Stay, Chelsea," she said, as she slipped outside. She gulped in a big breath of the clean night air. From her doorstep, she could see lights on in Jack's house. Beside her were the seven letterboxes at number 14, lit up by a streetlight. Terri walked towards them, turning down the driveway. She began to run, her tears cooling into salty smears on her cheeks from the breeze sighing restlessly through hedges and trees.

Jason was number 14D. The light was still on and

Terri could hear a familiar ad on TV. She knocked quietly. The whirr of the wheelchair came close to the door. "Who is it?" It was Jason's voice.

"Terri."

"Terri?" Jason asked, but he was already opening the door. "Come in. What's wrong?"

Inside was exactly the same layout as Chris's house, except Jason had lots of posters of bands and Chelsea soccer players on the wall. He was a Chelsea supporter too! Terri sat on the sofa. "You told me you were down this driveway if I needed your help."

"Yeah, I did."

"I'm too short. I can't stay in the squad. I'm going to pull out." Terri wiped her tears away angrily. She hated the fact that one person had the ability to upset her so much. Somehow, though, Antonia's voice had become the loudest at soccer and on Facebook. It didn't matter how many times Mum, Dad, Jules, Jack or Tim and teammates like Hera told her she was doing well, Antonia's voice drowned all of them out.

Jason wheeled himself nearer to the sofa. He reached down, picked up the TV remote and muted the sound. "Come with me," he said.

"Before we ring the police, Jack, is there anything you and Tim might know?" Terri's mother asked. "It's dark and I'm worried about her."

They were huddled around the table in Jack's house. Jack and Tim were in their pyjamas. Tim's dad was there too.

"There's this girl at soccer," Jack said. "She's been bullying her."

"We wanted to help, but she didn't want us to," Tim added.

"We should've done something, Timbo," Jack said.

"Jack, think carefully … there must be some kind of clue, something you know that might help us find her?" Jack's mother urged.

Tim felt a nervous feeling growing in his stomach. What if something bad had happened to Terri?

Jack leapt to his feet. "The fairy tale, remember Tim? Remember we were joking about the Seven Dwarfs. She's gone there, like …"

Tim stared at Jack. "Jack, this isn't—"

"No, remember how Jason told her to go there if she needed help?"

Tim nodded and stood up. "We have to go to Jason's."

Jason's eyes were level with hers in the low, wide hallway mirror. Terri's eyes were a different colour though: darker, like pools of black of ink. She blinked a few times. The light in here was very bright.

"What do you see?" Jason asked.

"Our reflections."

"Look closely." Jason spoke patiently, as if he had all the time in the world. Terri felt unsure, wondering if she might have interrupted his favourite TV programme.

"I'm short," Terri said.

"You're the same height as me."

"Yeah, but you're in a wheelchair, so you're sitting down."

"But this is as tall as I'll ever be now. I've become short, Terri. For the rest of my life, I'll be short."

Terri looked down at Jason's thin legs in the wheelchair. "Can you move your legs at all?"

"Nah. I used to lie in bed and tell my legs to move. I begged them, ordered them, yelled at them, but they stayed completely still."

Terri looked down at her legs. They were short and sturdy. Jason followed her gaze. "I've seen how you kick, Terri. I'll bet no other kid in this neighbourhood can kick like you."

Terri nodded slowly.

"I'm getting used to playing soccer as a shortie in a wheelchair. The important thing is, I'm playing soccer, Terri. That's all that matters. I deserve to play as much as anyone else."

"Do I deserve to play too?"

"What do you think?"

Terri nodded. "Yep, I do."

Jason smiled, pushing the wheels of his chair backwards to turn to face her. "You just remember that. That's the truth. You are as important as anyone else, whether you are large or small."

"Or in a wheelchair," Terri added.

"Or in a wheelchair," Jason agreed.

"I just wish Antonia would leave me alone. I wish there was some kind of magic to make her stop."

Jason smiled at Terri's reflection in the mirror. "You've got your own magic, Terri. For one thing, I've watched you play – and that's magic – but the real magic is that you're human. You're as equally human as anyone else."

"But Antonia thinks—"

"Terri, the truth's always there. You are her equal, even when Antonia treats you like you're nothing. Hang on to that truth, even if you can only glimpse it sometimes."

Terri nodded. "I'd better go, now. Thanks."

As they made their way from the hallway, the doorbell rang and they could hear voices outside. When Jason opened the door, Jack and Tim were there with Terri's parents.

"There you are!" her mother said, reaching out and hugging Terri to her.

"We were so worried," her father added, wrapping his arms around them both.

"Sorry, I should've rung you to let you know where she was," Jason said. "I didn't think."

"That would've been good," Terri's father said. "It's just a relief to know she's okay."

Jack turned to Tim. "Told you," he whispered. "The Seven Dwarfs. That's where Snow White goes."

Tim nodded. He thought of the wicked Queen and wondered if the girl from soccer was becoming a danger to Terri.

At the next squad practice, Terri kept what Jason had said firmly in her mind. Whenever she found herself thinking of Antonia, she reminded herself of the truth, that she had every right to be here. She'd been chosen to trial, just as Antonia had.

This was the last training before the rep team would be decided. Jules told them she and the other support coaches would finalise the list of those selected by the end of the weekend and an email would be sent out. Squad training was nearly over.

The truth stayed with her right through the skills practice. Thankfully, Antonia wasn't joining in the practice game, because she was wearing new boots and had developed painful blisters over the last hour. Watching from the sideline, Antonia's eyes were probably following Terri's every move, but Terri was determined to stay focussed on the fact that she had every right to be there.

Near the end of the game, Hera kicked the ball way off pitch and into the bushes surrounding the soccer fields. Terri, closest to the bushes, yelled, "I'll get it!" She ran through the scrub and bush looking for the ball. It had to be somewhere in this particular bit of bush, because she'd seen it go in there. Fortunately, the white ball was still visible in the fading evening light under a tangle of branches. "Got it," she said to herself. She crouched down and crawled under the bush to retrieve the ball.

Backing out, she stood up and began to run to re-join the game. Something tripped her though and she fell hard on her elbows, losing the ball, her face on the muddy earth, right next to a puddle. Might've been a broken branch or a tree root, she thought. She needed to look more carefully. At least she hadn't landed in the puddle. The ball had rolled ahead of her and she pushed up to her hands and knees to reach for it.

Two long legs stepped out from the bush and kicked the ball away from her grasp. The voice was Antonia's. "Oops, sorry, did I trip you? I just came to help you find the ball."

Looking up at Antonia, Terri struggled to keep the truth in her thoughts. She was too aware of the fact that she was alone with Antonia. Her thoughts became sludgy like the mud between her fingers. "I can get the ball without your help," she said.

"Can you? But you just let me kick it out of your hands!" Antonia looked down at Terri and laughed. "Are you scared, dwarfie? Look! Look at your scared little face in that puddle!"

A shaft of light peeked between the branches of the trees and bush so that Terri's reflection glimmered in the murky water. Behind her, Antonia said, "Your face is covered in mud!"

Stepping forward, Antonia's face was now reflected in the puddle too. A breeze shifted through the bush and the water rippled. Antonia's reflection wavered.

"You're scared," Terri said. "You're scared that you

won't get picked and I will." Terri stood up, brushed herself off and stepped forward to get the ball, but Antonia put her foot out and tripped her up again. This time though, Terri's head hit a rock as she fell. In that moment, everything – even the white ball – turned black.

Jules didn't phone the ambulance. Instead, she picked Terri up and drove her straight to the hospital herself. Hera had found her. She'd run into the bush as soon as she realised that Antonia had vanished from the sideline. It had been a shock to find Antonia crying, repeating Terri's name in between sobs in an attempt to wake her up. Hera phoned Terri's mother, while Jules drove.

Lying on the back seat of Jules' car, Terri opened her eyes. She assured Jules that she didn't need to go to the hospital. "It's okay," she said. "I just fainted. I feel fine now."

Jules glanced at Terri's pale face in the rear vision mirror. "You're going to hospital. You hit your head. Stop talking and rest, okay?"

The doctor listened to her heart, looked into her eyes, took her pulse, checked her blood pressure and inspected the bump on her head. She finally decided that Terri should stay overnight, just so that they could keep an eye on her in case she had concussion.

After the doctor had gone, Jules talked quietly with Terri's parents. "Antonia's out of the squad," she explained. "We can't have this sort of behaviour in a team. Rest assured, Terri will not have to put up with any of Antonia's nonsense in Japan."

Terri, eating yoghurt on the hospital bed, lowered her spoon and looked up. "I'm going to Japan?" she asked.

Jules turned to Terri. "I hadn't meant for you to hear that, but yes, Terri. You're definitely in the team, if you want to be. You were pretty much a certainty from the beginning."

"Yes!" Terri punched the air. "I'm in the team! Hear that, Mum? Dad? I'm in the team!"

The next day, home from hospital, Terri sat at the kitchen table catching up on homework. She could hear the Tui Street kids' voices long before they reached her door. Jack's voice was especially loud.

"The door's open!" Terri called.

Jack entered carrying a soccer ball. Ella had a box of cones and Tim had a container of chocolate ice cream in his hand. Gemma, Harry, Lucy and Louie came in behind them.

"We heard you were unconscious," Jack said, "and remember you told us you'd only wanna wake up to ice cream or a soccer ball? Well, here you are!"

Tim put the ice-cream container down on the table. "Got a spoon?"

"But I'm not unconscious anymore!" Terri said, laughing.

"Doesn't matter. You were," Jack said, rummaging in a drawer and finding an ice-cream scoop.

"Wanna play soccer after ice cream?" Harry asked.

Terri nodded, smiling. "Hey, but I want to tell you guys some good news," she said. "Jason too. Actually, I want to tell all of The Seven. Can we share the ice cream with them?"

"Will there be enough?" Tim asked.

"We've got some at home," Lucy said. "I'll run back and get it."

"We've got some too," Gemma said. "Boysenberry. I'll get that and meet you down there."

Gemma and Lucy left immediately on their ice-cream mission.

Louie smiled apologetically. "Sorry, guys. You know my Mum. She doesn't like biscuits or ice cream."

Jack picked up the ice-cream container. "Don't

worry, Louie, I've got the ice-cream scoop. I'll make sure you get a bit extra."

All seven neighbours at number 14 wanted to celebrate the news that Terri was in the national Under-15 team. Chris had marshmallows in his pantry and Bella went to look in her fridge for chocolate sauce. Cones were swapped for bowls and it became an ice-cream feast. As they ate and chatted, the discussion turned to the wheelchair soccer tournament. It was just over a week away.

"Twelve teams have signed up," Kepa said. "They're coming from all over the country."

"I can't wait to see you guys play against another team," Terri said. "You've just improved so much."

"You won't be able to yell rude things to the other teams like you do to us," Jack warned.

"Yeah. You'll get a red card," Tim agreed. "Do they have red cards in wheelchair soccer?"

No one knew.

"I'll check on the internet later," Tim said. "Just in case."

A couple of evenings later, the doorbell rang. Terri's father answered it. From the lounge, where Terri was curled up with Chelsea on a bean bag watching TV, she heard her father's low voice and some higher female voices. A moment later, her father came into the lounge. "Terri, would you turn off the TV, please. There's someone here who wants to see you."

Antonia and her mother came into the room and sat on the sofa opposite Terri. Terri's mother, who'd been snoozing with the newspaper on her lap, sat up straight, folding the newspaper away.

"Sorry to interrupt you," Antonia's mother said.

"No, not a problem." Terri's mother stood up. "Would you like a cup of tea?"

"No, thank you," Antonia's mother replied. "We won't stay long. We just came to see how Terri is."

Terri's mum sat down again. "Well, she's okay, considering her head hit a rock and knocked her out."

"Yes. Yes. Well, that's good." Antonia's mother fiddled with an earring.

The air filled with a silence so difficult to think in, that all Terri could do was pat Chelsea methodically and stare at her fur.

"Are you here to apologise?" Terri's dad asked.

"We really just wanted to see how Terri was, that's all," Antonia's mother said.

"You do realise this happened because your daughter tripped Terri up – twice – don't you?"

"None of us was there. It's difficult to know whose story is the truth without a witness."

"I know what happened. So does Antonia," Terri ventured quietly, still patting Chelsea, eyes fixed on her fur.

"This wouldn't have happened if she'd never been allowed to trial," Antonia said. Her cheeks had reddened. "Why would they let someone so young and small trial with us older girls? It's embarrassing and it shouldn't be allowed."

"The trials are about skill and technique, not age or size," Terri's mum said. "You have made Terri's life a misery with your cruel comments and bullying."

Antonia's mother gasped. "Bullying!"

"What would you call it?" Terri's dad said. "Assault?"

Antonia's mother gasped again, but said nothing.

Again there was an uncomfortable silence until, in a smaller voice, Antonia said, "I never really meant it to go this far."

"Don't snivel, Antonia," her mother replied. Looking at Terri's father, she said, "Antonia is a very good soccer player. Or she was until she got a bit older and other girls seemed to push ahead of her."

"I doubt they were pushing," Terri's mother said. "Sometimes others are just better at something. It's a fact of life."

"I told her she just had to keep trying." Terri's mother pursed her lips.

"I did try," Antonia said quietly. "I tried hard."

"Not hard enough. You needed to work harder."

A sniff was followed by another sniff, until Antonia stopped trying to disguise the fact that she was crying. "Mum, she's better than me!"

"Rubbish! You just didn't try hard enough. You're just as good as she is." Antonia's mother glared at Terri.

"But I'm not!" Antonia choked. Her face was wet with tears. "I'm not!"

Terri's mum stood up and came back with a box of tissues. "It must be exhausting trying to please your mum, Antonia," she said.

"I beg your pardon?" Antonia's mother stood up. "How dare you say that!"

Antonia blew her nose.

"Get up, Antonia. We're going home. Now." Antonia's mother pulled her daughter up by the arm. "Stand up, Antonia!"

Chelsea stood up worriedly at the woman's raised voice. Terri put a calming hand on her dog's back. She looked at Antonia, slowly responding to her mother's tugs on her arm. As her mother pulled her toward the door, Antonia turned around and looked at Terri. "I'm sorry. I never meant it to go this far," she said again. "And you *are* better than me."

"Will you come now, or do I have to drag you?" Antonia's mother demanded.

Antonia turned and walked out of the house with her mother. From inside the house, Terri and her parents could hear Antonia's mother scolding her loudly, even as they started the car and drove away.

The day of the wheelchair tournament arrived. There were a lot of people, both in and out of wheelchairs. The stadium had three indoor courts and each was alive with movement, squeals from wheelchair tyres, referee whistles, cheers and advice shouted from supporters in the stands. Terri sat with her parents and the Tui Street kids and their families.

The Seven won the first round of games, making it into the semi-finals. Jason had become a crowd favourite. His strength, speediness and skill with the ball had the crowd cheering and clapping every time he headed for goal.

Over the lunch break, Jason sidled up to Terri as she sat in the cafeteria. "My parents want to meet the coach," he said. "Mum and Dad, this is Terri."

Terri looked up from her sandwich, swallowing quickly so she could speak. "Hi," she said.

"You've done a great job, young lady," Jason's dad said.

"Jack and Tim helped me."

"Want to see some photos of your team in action?" Jason's mum asked.

"Yes, please," Terri answered.

Jason's mother's photographs were a series of moments that Terri had missed in the action-packed rush of the game. She'd photographed Bella's hair flying behind her as she sped to the ball. In another photo, Kepa was reaching up to catch the ball as it flew through the air. One funny one had Sula batting Bella's hair away from her face, as she tried to catch the ball with her other hand.

"I'll post them on Jason's Facebook page. Are you on Facebook?" Jason's mother asked.

Jason looked at Terri. "Are you still on Facebook?"

"Yep. I'm still on Facebook."

"She had a bad experience with someone on Facebook," Jason explained to his parents.

"Hmmm," Jason's father said. "Some people do stupid things."

"Like taking a corner too fast," Jason said.

Jason's dad nodded, squeezing Jason's shoulder gently.

The last five minutes of the final were so intense, that Terri bit three of her nails. She hadn't bitten her nails for a long time. The score was 5–4 to the opposition. Throughout the game, The Seven's main difficulty was the opposition's goalie, who did almost acrobatic tricks with his wheelchair. Regardless of which side people supported, they were all clapping at his amazing twists and spins to stop the ball as it headed towards the goal. When it came to the last five minutes, everyone was on the edge of their seat and cheering for their own team.

Jason had the ball. The goalie watched him like a hawk. He knew Jason was the one most likely to get a goal in the last few minutes. He'd already scored three for The Seven. Jason dribbled it like a basketball, swivelling his wheelchair so that it dodged his oncoming opponents. At an angle that looked almost impossible, Jason lifted his arm and shot the ball through the air, towards the goal. The crowd's cheers made the seats vibrate. Their arms were up, clapping and punching the air at Jason's accurate shot from such an unlikely angle.

At that very moment though, the goalie sped to the direction of the ball and twisted his body to the right so that his weight tipped the wheelchair onto its two right wheels. His long arm reached for the ball and, with a huge cheer from his supporters, he caught it. The whistle blew. The game was over. The Seven had come second in the tournament.

Although there was a little disappointment, it didn't take long for the laughter and teasing to start. "We'd have been okay if Bella's hair wasn't constantly impairing our vision," Kepa joked.

Bella snorted. "At least my hair isn't a health and safety risk. That rope of a plait of yours could knock someone out. It's actually, quite honestly, an offensive weapon."

The Tui Street kids asked to travel home with Jason in a mobility taxi van. As they drove through the dark streets, they began to plan for next year's tournament. They'd start practising earlier. Even through winter. Two practices a week.

Terri yawned and closed her eyes. Her short legs didn't touch the floor of the van, so she curled them up under her. Jason, too, closed his eyes.

When they turned into Tui Street Terri opened her eyes, sensing they were near home. At the bottom of the street she could see the seven letterboxes. She turned to Jason. He was awake now too. "You know what, Jason?" Terri said. "Coming second was pretty good."

Jason nodded. "Yep. Gives us something to work towards. We might win next year."

The driver stopped at the top of number 14's driveway to let the Tui Street kids out. Jack, Lucy and Louie had fallen asleep and the others had to shake them awake.

"Out, you lot," Jason said. "We all need to go to bed. Haven't done so much exercise in a long time."

"Don't forget you said we could skateboard down your ramp," Jack said, yawning. "Can we come this Saturday?"

"Saturday's good. Now, go home!"

Goodbyes were said, "Sleep well" was said, "See you tomorrow" too, until the friends headed homeward.

Terri slowed her steps up to the porch and turned to look back. The van had disappeared down the driveway. The moon was angular, like a slice of golden pie. To her right were the seven letterboxes. Along Tui Street, the lights of her friends' houses beamed comfortingly. She could hear their voices through the sleepy evening air, as they made their way to their homes.

It had been a long day. Time for bed.

Acknowledgements

Many thanks to Penny Scown and Lynette Evans at Scholastic for making this book happen, to the NZSA who gifted me a complete manuscript assessment with the clever Barbara Murison and to Scholastic and Storylines for the life-changing Tom Fitzgibbon Award. Thank you also to James George for his wise mentorship during the Masters in Creative Writing at AUT and to the AUT critique groups for their consistently insightful feedback.

I'm very grateful for the constant support of my good friends, the office 'flatties': Tui, Cordelia and Stephanie. Thank you also to Jacqui for her wise words and to my other dear friends for their love and support. I am grateful to my father and wonderful sisters, brothers, nieces and nephews for their encouragement of and belief in me. An enormous thank you (as large as the tree in Jack's front yard) to my husband, Steve, and our children, Sarah and Flynn, who supported me constantly as I wrote *Tui Street Tales*.

Finally, I am forever grateful to my mother, the bravest person I have ever met, who shared her love of words and stories with me, among many, many other things.

—Anne Kayes

Previous
Tom Fitzgibbon Award Winners

1996
Summer of Shadows
Iona McNaughton

1997
Dark Horses
Heather Cato

1998
2MUCH4U
Vince Ford

1999
The Stolen
Shirley Corlett

2000
Knocked for Six
Alison Robertson

2002
Mystery at Tui Bay
Janet Pates

2003
Shreve's Promise
Jullian Sullivan

2004
Stella Star
Brigid Freehan

2005
Mind Over Matter
Heather McQuillan

2006
Yo, Shark Bait
Vicki Simpson

2007
"Why I Hate School"
Kris Stanhope

2008
Salt River
Elizabeth Hegarty

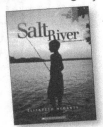

2009
Hollie Chips
Anna Gowan

2010
Super Finn
Leonie Agnew

2011
Iris's Ukulele
Kathy Taylor

2013
Night of the
Perigee Moon
Juliet Jacka

2014
How I Alienated
My Grandma
Suzanne Main

2015
Barking Mad
Tom E. Moffatt

*2001 and 2012 not awarded.

THE TOM FITZGIBBON AWARD

Storylines
Children's Literature Charitable Trust

This award was established in recognition of the outstanding contribution made by the late Tom Fitzgibbon to the growth and status of children's literature in New Zealand.

The award is made annually when merited, at the discretion of the Storylines Children's Literature Charitable Trust of New Zealand, and carries a monetary prize along with an offer of publication from Scholastic New Zealand Limited.